Elizabeth Bordley Gibson, Elizabeth Mifflin

Biographical Sketches of the Bordley Family of Maryland for their Descendants

Part First

Elizabeth Bordley Gibson, Elizabeth Mifflin

Biographical Sketches of the Bordley Family of Maryland for their Descendants
Part First

ISBN/EAN: 9783337031329

Printed in Europe, USA, Canada, Australia, Japan

Cover: Foto ©Raphael Reischuk / pixelio.de

More available books at **www.hansebooks.com**

BIOGRAPHICAL SKETCHES

OF THE

BORDLEY FAMILY,

OF MARYLAND.

FOR THEIR DESCENDANTS.

PART FIRST.

BY

MRS. ELIZABETH BORDLEY GIBSON,

EDITED BY HER NIECE,

ELIZABETH MIFFLIN.

PHILADELPHIA:
PRINTED BY HENRY B. ASHMEAD,
Nos. 1102 AND 1104 SANSOM STREET.
1865.

ELIZABETH BORDLEY GIBSON.

A SLIGHT sketch of the writer of the within memoir, certainly will require no apology. It is given as a mere outline, leaving to a future time, something more minute and
more worthy of her, which may be culled from her
numerous papers and letters.

Elizabeth Bordley Gibson, daughter of John Beale
and Sarah Bordley, was born October 21st, 1777. Her
parents resided on Wye Island, Maryland, half of which
was owned by her father. They retreated to Annapolis,
the metropolis of the State, in consequence of the too near
approach of the British army, and there, Elizabeth Bordley was born, amid the booming of cannon and the cheers
of the people for the surrender of Burgoyne and his forces
to General Gates at Saratoga.

She was most carefully educated solely by her parents
at Wye, until she was thirteen years old. They then removed to Philadelphia; she was placed under the care of
the most competent teachers, and at this time, she became
a constant visitor in the family of General Washington,
having masters with the granddaughter of Mrs. Washington, the celebrated Nelly Custis. Lessons were taken,

sometimes at General Washington's in Market Street, sometimes at Mr. Bordley's. It has been asked, did General Washington ever dance after he became President? With a look, beaming with pleasure, my aunt often told of his kindness in joining them in their simple country dances after the public levee was over.

Elizabeth Bordley's talents were of a superior order, and with the study of her own language, every one of them which she possessed was cultivated; music, painting, foreign languages and composition, until she had acquired a most highly finished education; unexcelled in those days, and rarely in these. She grew up to womanhood, everything the fondest parents could desire; affectionate, dutiful, prudent, correct in every principle, with highly polished manners, combined with great modesty and diffidence of her own powers; she was a fine musician, instrumental and vocal, an exquisite sketcher of scenery, and an elegant writer. This last she retained until a short time before the close of her long life, and letters of that date might be shown as models of fine composition. Congress was in session in Philadelphia when she entered into society, and consequently the great men of our country, and eminent foreigners congregated there. Miss Bordley soon became a distinguished belle; her tall, fine figure, handsome poetical face, her highly refined manners and various accomplishments, placed her among the most prominent and most admired in the brilliant circle in which she moved.

Her father's death in 1804, and her mother's long protracted debility, withdrew her from the fashionable world, and quietly, for many years, she attended the declining years of her mother, having the additional sorrow of losing her brother, Mr. Mifflin, two years before their mother's death; one, to whom both she and her mother looked for advice and affectionate care. In these days of leisure and repose, she became an ardent lover of her Bible, and stored her mind and heart with its glorious truths, and learned habitually to put her whole trust in the mercy and support of her heavenly Father and her Redeemer. In all the trials of after-life, this rock of support never failed her. In May, 1817, her mother being dead, she married James Gibson, Esq., and led a life, as most persons do, of checkered happiness and sorrow. She was a widow some years, and sank to rest on the bosom of her God, August 23d, 1863.

A few weeks before the death of my aunt, Mrs. Gibson, she wrote to me while I was in the country, July 31st, 1863:—"Some 20 or 30 years ago, I pleased myself by writing all I could recollect of my dear father's life and connections, and without a thought of having it printed; but a few years ago, some friends, to whom I gave a glimpse of it, insisted I ought to finish it for taking its place in the 'National Gallery of Portraits.' * * * I owed it to my father's memory. * * * After this, I made up my mind to have it ready for the printer. * * * Now I am too old and infirm to undertake copying and preparing it. But, what say you to doing this for me? you would be doing good for me, and perhaps some others. * * * I think we may feel it a bond of union to us."

I willingly assented, and a subsequent short conversation confirmed our agreement. Before it could be placed in my hands, she was no more. And now I present *all* she has written; no omissions were required, and but few trifling corrections of words have been made.

E. M.

March 12*th*, 1864.

Dedicated,

WITH

Affectionate Congeniality and Kindred Regard,

TO THE

DESCENDANTS OF THE BORDLEY FAMILY,

By their Relative and Well Wisher,

THE AUTHOR.

Jan. 1826.

TO THE READER.

THE desire to trace some knowledge of those relations who have preceded us, is so natural to the cultivated heart, that it is unnecessary to form excuses for it. All who have been habituated by the blessings of a good education, to love the ties of consanguinity, to respect and cherish the endearing names of father, mother, brother, sister, &c., will feel it needless to analyze the sentiment—they know, and value the truth of the poet's thoughts:

> " 'Tis man alone that joy descries
> With forward, and, reverted eyes."—GRAY.

In the exercise of this "reverting" privilege, I have employed some leisure hours in collecting together such scattered evidences of past times, as throw a ray of light, though but too faint, on our family history.

The pursuit has greatly interested me, and if the following imperfect result may meet the eye of any of my present or future kindred, who own a congenial feeling, I shall not have busied my feeble pen in vain.

This hope shall fondly impel me "forward" in my task, and, Gentle Reader! as this little manuscript is not to wander beyond the Bordley descendants, I will confess

myself one of the same lineage—perhaps you are my own
dear second, third, or fortieth cousin, and taking it for
granted that you are gracious, kind, and altogether
amiable, I entrust this my friendly bequest, to your lenity
and discretion.

E. B. G.

PHILADELPHIA, *January*, 1826.

PART FIRST

SKETCHES OF THE LIVES

OF

THOMAS BORDLEY AND ARIANA, HIS WIFE.
STEPHEN BORDLEY,
WILLIAM BORDLEY,
ELIZABETH BORDLEY,
JOHN BORDLEY,
THOMAS BORDLEY,
MATTHIAS BORDLEY.

PART SECOND

JOHN BEALE BORDLEY.

BIOGRAPHICAL SKETCHES, &c.

THOMAS BORDLEY.

The earliest knowledge we trace of this family is, that they were of Yorkshire, England, and were there very respectably established; that they were prosperous at an early period, and afterwards tossed upon the shore of adversity by one of those waves which the tide of time deals, sooner or later, to most of the families of the earth. In their different generations, several of them were regularly educated clergymen, and men of learning;* one of these became a Prebendary of St. Paul's, London. Letters of a later period, from 1711 to 1725, are now before us, from the Rev. William Bordley, residing then in Westmoreland; they allude familiarly to various family circumstances, although too incidentally to give us, of this distant day. full acquaintance with them. In one he mentions having lately made a journey into Yorkshire, to inquire after some aged relations there, and to look at the village settled by his ancestors, and called by their name; that one

---

* We have a commonplace book of one of these, very old, which confirms this circumstance of their having learning amongst them. (Note A.) In Pott's "Gazetteer of England and Wales," published in 1810, London, are the following articles:—" *Boardley*—Staincliffe wap. *Yorkshire*, 7 m. N. E. from Settle." " *Boardley Hall*—Staincliffe wap. *Yorksh.*, 6 m. E. from Settle."

2

of them had formerly owned a Hall, or country-seat, near the town, but that things were much changed. He refers his nephew, for a more particular account of this place, to a work published about the year 1700 or 1702, entitled " Index Villaris."

In one of these letters the Rev. Wm. B. mentions that "about 200 years ago"—*i.e.* about the year 1500—one of their family was sent from that county as Sheriff of London.   In another letter he alludes to the altered circumstances of their family before his birth—and that his father had been in his day the "only man of letters" left amongst them.   His brother it was who was Prebendary of St. Paul's Church, London,—which circumstance proves the previous high standing of the family.

At the time of these letters from the Rev. Wm. Bordley, there were several female descendants still living in Yorkshire, whom he mentions as relations; two of them were his nieces, respectable old ladies, who, though in reduced circumstances, were considered as being entitled to the deference and respect which they received.   They corresponded with their great nephew, Stephen Bordley, and he made them a visit in 17—.

Thomas Bordley, the more immediate object of our attention, was born in Yorkshire, about the year 1682; he was the youngest son of Stephen Bordley, the above-mentioned Prebendary, and nephew of the Rev. Wm. Bordley, from whose correspondence we have quoted.   He came over to America in 1694, with an elder brother,* who was a clergyman.   They first settled in Kent County, Eastern Shore of Maryland.   Thomas was then about twelve years

* Stephen Bordley, of Kent County, Maryland.

old; he had lately lost his father; his family in England thought him well provided for under the care of a brother; but that brother himself probably had difficulties to contend with, for, after finishing his own good plain education, it appears he could do nothing more for him.

Then it was, that Thomas evinced the manly energy of his disposition, and adopted the nobly independent part of acting for himself, and urging his own way towards those high advantages in knowledge which he was ambitious of attaining. Young as he was, totally unknown, unsupported, unprovided, he went alone to Annapolis, the capital of the Province, and headquarters of every distinction it afforded. Like a being, dropped down from some other sphere, possessing nothing but an honest countenance, with good language and penmanship, he stepped at once into the busy little world of that city, trusting in Providence and the energies of his own mind. There he contrived to establish himself firmly, humbly at first, but with higher views and by close application of his own mind, calling upon all its resources for ingenuity, industry, good humor and patience, he qualified and prepared himself for the law. It is not meant that he effected this without enlightening aid from others—friends he found, but he made them friends by his own good sense and good conduct: at the same time, that he showed respect for them and their advice, he evinced respect for himself and a desire to be independent. Facts speak volumes for a young man thus situated. In due time he was admitted to practice, and soon, wonderfully soon, became eminent. He applied to that profession not merely with a view to profit; had he aimed at wealth only, he would never have acquired what

is infinitely superior to it, a meritorious high standing in
society.   He gained what he most desired—a legal character worthy of the highest trusts.   Young stranger as he
was, he was soon distinguished and respected as a rising
character, of good abilities, already learned in his profession, making conscientious integrity his guide, and industry his handmaid.

The history of individuals, and judicious observations on
the world, both alike prove that man's best interests here
are founded on the religious moral principle.   Sound elementary views, courageously sustained, have formed everything that has ever been admirable in the human character.   This truth was clearly evinced in him whose life we
are tracing.   Mr. Bordley sustained an ample and steady
course of forensic success, of private respectability and of
public honor, in all which he was the fabricator of his own
fame, and that fame was to the last, fair and unsullied.
Shall we pause to reflect how this was accomplished ? Not
by the designing arts or plodding contrivances of a feeble
mind—nor yet, by the suggestions of a powerful mind,
guided by false and insidious views, but by superior capacity, firmly directed to honest designs, based on the substantial and time-conquering rights of a Christian, of one
who acknowledged himself accountable to a superior Master and nobler motive, than can be found in the powers or
the prosperity of this world.   Thus it was, that Thomas
Bordley made himself an exemplary and honored character.   His talents were indeed of the first order, and wealth
rewarded his industrious application of them, yet without
the Inward Guardian which he consulted, he would not
have added to his possessions, that high feeling of respect

which was shown him through life, and is still paid to his memory.

He was considered the first lawyer of his day; his opinions were sought with eagerness, not only in the then Province of Maryland, but also in the neighboring Provinces, especially in Pennsylvania and New York. Letters are now before us, expressing thanks from distinguished persons to this favorite lawyer, and they also prove that some, now amongst us, descendants of the wealthy of those days, owe their present possessions to the skillful efforts of Thomas Bordley of Maryland.

The weight and influence of his character in the flourishing and distinguished community of Annapolis could not fail to bring him forward in a political career also—his firm and independent principles sustained him through many a colonial trouble of that day. Amongst other evidence of this, it is seen in his private correspondence with his Uncle William Bordley, the clergyman in England, before mentioned, which, on the part of the American, as Thomas then was, breathes the free spirit of a vigorous mind, ardently claiming its adopted country's rights, yet proving itself true and submissive to the love of order, without which nothing can be done rightly.

It is not to be supposed that in a period of dissensions, rivalships, and public disputes, such as Mr. Bordley encountered in those unsettled times, he could escape from difficulties and contests with the selfish and the envious. Few indeed, if any, who are above mediocrity, can pass through life undisturbed by the fallacious views of others. But it was a marked trait in his character, and stands now on record before us as a tribute of justice from his pastor,

2*

that he forgave his enemies. When taking the communion for the last time, previous to his departure for England, he requested the minister particularly to understand, " that he left the country in full charity, without the least ill will to any person."

His greatest trials of patience appear to have occurred whilst he was a member of the General Assembly. He was a strenuous and active supporter of the rights of the Colonies, and injured both his health and his estate by giving himself up to his patriotic efforts, "especially," as the document before us says, " by his extraordinary application to public business during a long Session of the General Assembly."

In 1715, Thomas Bordley Esq., was appointed Attorney-General. In this office he acquitted himself faithfully and well, and held it eleven years, that is, until the period of his death.

He was twice married. His first wife was Rachel Beard, of Annapolis; she brought him many children, but only four survived the state of infancy, viz., Stephen, William, Elizabeth, and John. Of this wife we only know that she was a good woman, much beloved by her husband and family. She died in 1722.

His second wife was the widow Frisby, whose maiden name was Ariana Vanderheyden; of her we shall speak in a separate chapter. They were married Sept. 1st, 1723. She brought him three sons, viz., Thomas, Matthias, and John Beale, the last, born four months after his father's death.

After suffering long with the growing disease which was to terminate his valuable life, he was at last induced to go

to London for surgical aid from the famous Dr. Chessel-
den, but the operation for removing the cause of his disease,* proved fatal, and he died soon after it, perfectly
sensible of his approaching dissolution, and, making various
arrangements for it, he breathed his last October the 11th,
1726, O. S., at the age of 43—a short, but well-spent
life, a life strongly marked by integrity of purpose, energy
in pursuit, and ability in execution.

We have exhibited a slight sketch of his success and
high standing in Maryland, both as a lawyer and a public
character. Of this, the public records of those times, as well
as his note-books, letters, &c., all bear witness. We are
more deficient in evidences of the private incidents and
qualities of his domestic character, but we know that nothing has ever appeared casting the slightest shade on his
venerated memory.

Various public testimonials of respect were shown on
the intelligence of his death reaching Annapolis. A sermon was delivered on the occasion,† and, according to the
manner of showing religious respect to the memory of the
good and distinguished of those times, the church was
hung with black, and its officers and most of the congre-
gation habited in mourning. In this sermon, which we
have before us, the preacher says: "The more I consider
him (Thos. Bordley, Esq.) the more he gained upon my
admiration and respect. I found frequent occasion to believe him to be a man of great probity and sincerity. In
the progress of my inspection, I found him to be a very
rigid lover of justice, insomuch, that he would not spare

* The Stone.
† By the Rev. John Humphreys, Rector of St. Anne's Church, Annapolis.

even his most intimate friends when they committed any transgression within his cognizance, in his company or hearing, and yet none more frank and cheerful in conversation, as well as innocent. Those whom he thought worthy of his friendship, he would serve with pleasure and with great resolution. In short, he was a person in whom I could observe no evil either in practice or inclination. He was a true and dutiful son to the church, and a zealous defender of her constitutions. * * * * He was a constant attending companion at the altar. * * * * In fine, he was an excellent husband, a most tender parent, a good master, a faithful and diligent performer of all the business in which he was engaged in human life. And he was a good patriot to his country, in the service of which he very much spent himself and injured his health."

Elegies and epitaphs also commemorated this event, which seemed felt as a public loss. Their *verse* will not well bear quotation ; we will only copy one passage.

> " Mourn, Senators ! your heads with cyprus crown,
> And let the Bar with sable weeds hang down ;
> The leading member in your house is dead,
> To Heaven's imperial court for justice fled ;
> But Bordley's name, immortal as his soul,
> Will never die whilst Sol does time control."

In person, Mr. Bordley was tall, stout and athletic. A full-length portrait of him, in a long wig and flowing robe, taken by Hesselias, portrait painter at Annapolis, represents him rather thin and pallid. It was painted a short time before he sailed for England, when he was wasted by a painful disease. The countenance is intelligent and mild, with a high, full forehead, penetrating eyes, and a playful expression around its firm and manly mouth, which, knowing the character, we may say, indicates the good man.

He left a large estate to be equally divided among his seven children, as they came of age, including the same apportionment for the one not then born, and providing handsomely for his widow.

This will gives strong evidence of what has been above observed, his high sense of justice and his independence of mind in acting accordingly, for in those days, an equal division among children was not customary, and the general system of laws and government was adverse to it. In reflecting on his life and character, we are compelled to observe, that his was not a common mind, and that it was improved on the immutable principles of wisdom and truth.

ARIANA VANDERHEYDEN.

She was the fourth daughter of Matthias Vanderheyden, of New York; described in an old memorandum before us, as being "related to the Schuyler family, of that city;" and as a "plain man, respected more for the goodness of his heart, than for his greatness." His wife, Anna Margaretta, was the daughter of Colonel Augustine Hermann, (or Harmann,) originally from Prague, in Germany, from whence he was driven by the religious persecutions of the times; he owned the large and valuable tract of land in Cecil County, Maryland, to which he gave the name of

Bohemia-Manor, and he named Bohemia River; he also possessed several other tracts of land in that State, and in Delaware; the ground where New Castle now stands was entirely his.

When Matthias Vanderheyden married Miss Hermann, he removed from New York to Maryland, and settled on part of Bohemia-Manor. He there raised several sons and daughters—the sons all died without progeny; the four daughters inherited that large estate. Of these four daughters

THE ELDEST, Jane V., married a Mr. Couts, merchant of Scotland, where she died, leaving a son, Hercules Couts, who married and died, leaving a son James Couts, (he was in Braddock's Army, with Sir John Sinclair, Quartermaster-General, who was related to the Couts' family,) and a daughter, Margaret Couts, who married Alexander Corbet, of Scotland.

The second, Francina V., married a Shippen; they had one child, Margaret Shippen, who married a Jekyll, and left a son, John Jekyll, and two daughters—the youngest of these daughters, Margaret Jekyll, married Col. Chalmers, who took her to England, where she died. They left several sons and daughters; one son, George Chalmers, who distinguished himself both in law and letters—the literary world owes several valuable histories to his pen—amongst them, a very learned Memoir of Mary Queen of Scots, Annals, &c.

Francina, after the death of her husband Shippen, married Col. Hynson, of Chestertown, Maryland, where she died, aged ninety years.

The third, Augustina V., married James Harris, of Maryland; they had one son, Matthias Harris. She died in 1775, aged upwards of ninety years.

The fourth, Ariana V., married first James Frisby, by whom she had three daughters, viz.:

1st. SARAH FRISBY, born December, 1714, who married John Brice; they had four sons, John,* James, Benedict, and Edmund Brice, and five daughters.

1. Of whom, Ariana Brice, married Dr. Ross.

2. Sarah Brice, married John Henderson.

3. Ann Brice.

4. Elizabeth Brice, married first Lloyd Dulany — then Walter Dulany; they left a son, Grafton Dulany, (still living,) and two daughters, Mary and Sarah; Mary married Mr. Rogers;† 5th daughter married Major Leitch; they had a son, James Leitch, and a daughter, Sarah Leitch, who married John Addison; they have many children.

2d. Margaret Frisby, who married William Harris; they had a son, who died childless.

3d. Augustina Frisby married Dr. Daniel Cheston; their son, James Cheston, married Miss Galloway, of West River, [where she is still

* This John Brice was the father of Judge Nicholas Brice, who is therefore the grandson of Sarah Frisby, Mrs. Brice, the half-sister of my father, J. B. B.

† Mr. Henry Rogers, since dead; his widow in Baltimore, in 1834.

(in 1826) living; has a son, James Cheston, and a daughter, Frances Cheston]—of their son Daniel there is no account—their daughter, Frances C., married Mr. Bentzley, of England; [in 1794, they were living in London.]

Ariana Vanderheyden's second husband was Thomas Bordley, Esq. They were married September 1st, 1723, and settled, of course, in his house, near the State House, Annapolis. Here were born their three sons, Thomas, Matthias, and John Beale—the last, the only one of Mr. Bordley's seven children, whose progeny now survives. While they resided together in Annapolis, Mrs. Ariana Bordley still further established that character for excellence by which she had been previously distinguished, which has been liberally acknowledged by all who ever knew her, and is still handed down with affectionate pride by her posterity.

She was remarkably handsome, both in features and figure; her person, air, and manner have been described as possessing a native dignity that forbade familiarity, while it gave a more winning and attractive charm to a gentle sprightliness peculiarly her own. Her conduct through life was in harmony with this exterior; she was admired, respected, and beloved. It was said, by one of her sons, within the recollection of the writer, and in the presence of a friend who confirmed the remark, that "no one could forget the mild sparkle of her eye, nor the sweet tones of her voice, nor the dignity of her deportment; and that no parent could bestow a better wish on a daughter than that she might resemble her in everything!"

Her conduct in all respects was exemplary, but particularly so in the character of a step-mother, and of this there exists clear evidence in the letters of her step-son, Stephen Bordley; from which we shall presently give extracts in our sketch of his life.

Ariana's third husband, married November, 1728, was Edmund Jenings, Esq., of Annapolis, where they resided until 1737, when he took her to England. She was there inoculated for the small-pox, of which she died in April, 1741.

Mr. Jenings came back to Annapolis, and held some distinguished offices, but afterwards revisited England. where he died in 1756. They left a son, Edmund Jenings. and a daughter, Ariana Jenings. Their son, born in 1731. went to England with his parents, and remained there: completed his education, and entered on the practice of the law. But being an acknowledged friend to America throughout her troubles, he turned his attention to more animating subjects than the law, and was afterwards employed by her new Government in various Embassies abroad—a proof of their confidence in his principles: although he never returned to his native country. He resided principally in England, where he was highly respected, and his society sought by some of the first people there, both in rank and literature.* He lived to the advanced age of *eighty-eight*, "alert and vigorous both in mind and body" beyond his years, and died in 1819.†

* The writer received an entertaining account of him and his peculiarities, from Lord Henry Steuart, when in this country, as Secretary to Mr. Liston, in 1797.

† See a London publication entitled "Annual Obituary and Biographical Notices"—for "1821." In the Philadelphia Library, No. 4978, October; article "Edmund Jenings."

3

Their daughter, Ariana Jenings, married John Randolph, of Virginia; brother to the celebrated Peyton Randolph. They had one son, Edmund Randolph, some time Secretary of State, appointed by General Washington, when President; and two daughters, Ariana and Susan; one of whom married a Mr. Grimes, who took her to England; the other married a Mr. Wormeley, who took her, also, to England; the latter left a son, now Rear Admiral Wormeley, married and settled at Boston, 1826.*

STEPHEN BORDLEY.

Stephen, eldest son of the Thomas and Rachel Bordley before mentioned, was born at Annapolis, Maryland, in 1709. He was early sent to England, for education, and soon after his father's death, he entered there on the study of the law, as his father, just before his death, advised him. In his letters to his step-mother, and other friends, on the subject of his profession, and his future course of life, he shows a strong mind, vigorous in reasoning; and equally docile and amiable in deference and respect to his experienced friends and guardians. This good sense early appeared; while yet a youth at school in England, he wrote to his great-uncle, the Rev. Wm. Bordley, clergyman, before mentioned, in a way which excited the old gentleman's surprise; and in one of his letters to Stephen's father, dated Westmoreland, 1725, speaking of his "young

* Returned to England and in the Royal Navy.

kinsman," Stephen having lately written to him, he adds, " that letter contains these remarkable words, viz.: 'all my aim is to oblige my friends, which I can never better do than by doing the best for myself.' I've reason to congratulate you upon the number of your children, since 'tis scarce possible such parts, well employed, should ever want bread, in your world!"*

But although Stephen's spirited turn of mind thus early showed itself, nothing could be more affectionately respectful than his whole conduct towards his guardians and elder friends. His habit of keeping a letter-book, commenced immediately after his arrival in England, gives now an opportunity of catching various traits which mark his character—and his was a character that showed itself manfully, and did not leave itself to be discovered by chance or surmise—foibles and mistakes, *all* came to light! Its predominant tone, whilst he was in England, appears to have been an earnest and passionate attachment to his native country, and a correspondent eagerness to return to it. He remained in England ten years, first in going through various schools, afterwards in close study of the law for four years with an attorney; afterwards for several years in the Temple. He appears to have taken a moderate share of amusement; and not to have neglected any of his social duties. Among the latter, were attentions to several elderly aunts and cousins of the Bordley family, in

---

* In the close of this old gentleman's letter there is the following sensible rule of conduct. He mentions that an " Ancient Seat" (with many advantages) is likely to be " sold soon for £9 or 10,000; but, qua supra nos, nihil ad nos. A sufficiency with contentment is both the satisfaction and delight of him . . . . who subscribes himself your truly affectionate Uncle,

W. B."

Yorkshire; in whose affairs he took an affectionate interest, remarkable in so young a man; he supported a
steady intercourse with them whilst in England, and continued the correspondence by letter, after his return
home.

For this event he was impatient, but he had resolved to
reap the full harvest of instruction that he had entered
upon, and to hasten the wished for period of return, he
labored with a zeal proportioned to the steady ardor of
his character. Speaking in one of his letters of his own
country, he says: "I should be much troubled ever to see
that country without being capable of serving it. It was
for that purpose I was sent out here; and, therefore, to
return without so doing would be adverse to the intention
of my father." * * "Unless you give me so plentiful
an education, that I may be able to serve others as well
as myself, it will all be in vain, &c." "* * If you still
propose that I sh^d see you without learning some business,
I cannot forbear saying it will be an action much like that
of a countryman, who pulled his fruit before it was ripe,
and thereby lost the profit of it. I should certainly be
very willing to see you and my other friends, if I was
qualified as fully as my father intended; but since it is not
so, let me prevail with you to lay aside so much of that
tenderness belonging to mothers (if such is the reason) as
to allow me time to learn some business in London, for no-
where better can business be learnt. It was, a little before his operation, the opinion of my father, that I should
be fittest for the law—it is also the opinion of Mr. Hunt:
what I myself have the greatest inclination to, and what
will be of most service to my country, &c." To Mr. Beale,

an excellent friend of the family, and the executor of his father's estate, he writes thus: "I heartily thank you for your kind advice; you need not doubt but I shall endeavor to follow it, considering that

'My Father's merit sets me up to view,
And shews me in the fairest point of light
To make my virtues or my faults conspicuous.'*

As you are now the chief manager of our affairs, I beg you will take the trouble to advise mother concerning the future part of my life. I should be very willing to see her and my other friends, was I qualified to do them any service, but I have not yet been to learn any business, &c."

These were written before affairs at home were quite settled, and show the ardor and impatience of a youth of eighteen, who, to use his own words, considers "all his future happiness as hanging on the present moment!" To say truth, and we should not be worthy of our task if we did not, impatience seems to have been one of Stephen's foibles; but the candor and artlessness with which he betrays it, should disarm censure, especially when we find that it never impelled him to unjust conduct; nor ever prevented the magnanimity with which he often acknowledged himself mistaken.

About the same period he expressed himself thus in writing to his Reverend Uncle William: "You seemed pleased with the provision my father hath made for us; which indeed, were it but in England, would be a vast estate; but as it is, the best of that land is not worth above 20s. or 22s. pr. acre. But, however, I am content,

* Addison's Cato.

and wonder how he could get so much; always having
enemies and enviers, who endeavored to subvert his under-
takings; which was without dispute, a great hinderance to
him." Soon afterwards we find him writing to thank his
step-mother for her generous acquiescence in his plans,
and also to assure her that he shall "not credit anything
to the dispraise of her marriage ;" on the contrary, " I am
confirmed in the belief of Mr. Jening's good-will to our
family; and as to yours, I was long ago having experienced
it."

For his step-mother, he appears to have had a truly
filial affection, founded on admiration of her virtues. In a
letter to one of his aunts in England, he mentions some
conduct of hers with high approbation, and adds, "but she
is a step-mother of the first rank." In writing to herself,
he implores her "by the tenderness she has always shown
him, &c." Her third marriage seems to startle him at first,
and calls forth somewhat of his turn to satire, but he be-
comes quite reconciled to it. While yet but nineteen, he
writes to her thus: "I perceive there are some who, since
my father's death, have dared to exert themselves, and
undertake what they never dared to do whilst he was
living; which shows their meanness of spirit, and gives his
successor an insight into their characters, and thereby an
advantage in managing them. You may rely on it, I shall
take all opportunities of improving myself, that I may be
able in time to serve my friends, and especially yourself (if
ever you sh⁴ be so unhappy as to want it,) who hath put so
good an opportunity of improvement into my hands." The
latter part refers to her great generosity in taking on herself the expenses of his education.

His first attention to the law was with a respectable attorney in London, selected by his guardian, Mr. Hunt, a most estimable man. He engaged for a course of study of five years, for two hundred guineas; with the privilege of withdrawing at the end of four years, if he chose. At the same time his brother William is engaged by their guardian, Mr. Hunt, to a merchant for three hundred guineas.

It does not appear at what time exactly Stephen entered the Temple, perhaps on his return to England. With his teacher, the attorney, he seems well pleased, expressing himself thus to his reverend uncle, date 1729: "I am now at Mr. Page's, an attorney in Austin-fryers, near the Royal Exchange. I am articled for five years, to leave at four if I think fit—where, I thank God, nothing is wanting to render me as completely happy as this world can admit."

His undeviating attachment to home is feelingly and naturally displayed in his letters to his own family, both in America and England, and also to his boyish and youthful friends on this side of the Atlantic; amongst whom were two of his quondam schoolfellows, Edward and James Tilghman, of Maryland. This friendship, renewed when they entered on the busy stage of life together, was strengthened with each succeeding year of their lives; some of the gay and easy letters which passed between them still exist, and mark the genuine and gentlemanly frankness of their mutual regard.

His brother William, not liking the profession chosen for him, was recalled home, and left England in 1731.

Some extracts from Stephen's subsequent letters to him

will show both his affection for his brother, and the sound reflections he was, even so young, capable of forming.

LONDON, *Apl.* 5, 1731.

" DR WILL :

Since your departure, I have been under several disappointments ; for having several times thought with myself that I had not seen you for a long time, I have, in order to go to see you at your school, frequently half dressed myself before I have discovered my mistake. By this you may see that I often think of you, &c."

" Inclosed is a letter from your Aunt ——; you'll there see that she recommends to you above all things a due observance of your duty to your great Creator—herein I also join with her, and make it also my request that you would do so ; but since she hath not told you wherein that duty consists, for want of knowing which you may possibly fall into a very great, and I fear common, error in that point, I shall endeavor, in 2 or 3 words, to put it in your power to avoid it. The error is this : some men imagine they have done their duty to their Creator when they have gone to Church twice a day & muttered over a few prayers, and perhaps heard one or two sermons, without ever desiring what they seem to pray for, or designing to live up to the rules laid down in those sermons ; but this is so far from being a due performance of one's duty, or being anywise acceptable to the Supreme Being, that 'tis on the contrary a direct affront to him, as 'tis supposing him to be so stupid as to afford his blessings to any that ask them, tho' in so slovenly a manner, as if they were indifferent whether they obtained what their words seem to request of him, or no. This is an error the * * * * have most unhappily fallen into, & which you must as much as possible avoid. In short, go constantly to Church, and whether you pray or hear, let the one be done with the greatest desire of obtaining what you ask, and with a resolution of doing your endeavor to that end; and the other with the like resolution of living up to those rules there laid down to govern your actions. Observe this, dear Will, as you have a regard to the difference between a happy & a miserable eternity.

"A man is neither a better nor a worse man, nor will any one of common sense think him so, for any, even extraordinary virtues or flagrant vices, [& much less for any accidental circumstances in life,] which any of his family may have been noted for, for these things are wholly personal, and cannot extend to any but such as are the immediate possessors of them.

"Think on your present course of life. How will it enable you to serve your Country, your friends, or even to keep yourself from starving? 'Tis a matter well worth your consideration."

In the spring of 1733, he quitted the attorney's office, and instantly prepared for his voyage home, towards which his heart rebounds with the elasticity of a spring long repressed! In the June of that year, he dates a round of letters to his friends and relations in England, from Annapolis; informing them of his " safe arrival," finding " all well," his "reception being as agreeable as he could wish," &c., &c., all in high spirits and his wonted jocose manner. At the same time, by the list of law books that he orders sent out to him, he proves himself much in

earnest in his law vocation. Before the expiration of a
year, we find him engaged in a lawsuit with the Lord
Baltimore, and in consequence of it, he returns back to
England in the spring of 1734, in company with his step-
father, Mr. Jenings, and his half-brother, Thomas Bordley,
then about ten years old, who was taken for his education,
and put to school without loss of time.

Then follow letters expressive of lively affection to his
sister Elizabeth, his " dear Bett," with many gallant and
complimentary allusions to the charming ladies of Annapolis ; and some half-hid expressions, which look very
much like a particular attachment—but to whom, is not
told ! His letters dated on board ship, mention Miss Carroll as being of their party ; he closes most of them with
assurances that " Mr. Jenings, Miss Carroll, and Tom are
well," and to his step-mother, with his accustomed ease
and affection, he says, " good company, good weather,
plenty, & an easy ship, cannot but render our passage
pleasant," &c.

While in England on this occasion, he took chambers in
the Temple, with the view to advance and perfect himself
in the law during his stay. While a young man, he showed
himself remarkably alert and anxious to take advantage of
time and opportunity, for further benefit ; and not to sacrifice this judicious system, for mere idle gratification of the
present moment: yet he enjoyed life—nobody more ! He
appears always happy and full of playful humor, but he
made it a point in his own mind, not to permit the present
to beguile him of the future ; he sent his thoughts forward,
more than is very common, even to well educated youth.

A few more extracts from his letters will show him more

completely than any other language. Writing to his aunts, who resided in a distant part of England, he has occasion to lament for them, some difficulties in their affairs, and adds: "I am in hopes this will not produce discontent; the possessions of this life are so precarious, and in themselves such trifles, that none but lunaticks or fools would suffer much uneasiness at parting with them; and as I have no reason to think you either one or the other, I persuade myself you bear your loss as you should do." In another letter, speaking of his step-mother's family in Annapolis, he says:

"There is scarce anything upon earth I more desire, than to be with that agreeable family: which desire, together with the difference between this most unwholesome, muggy climate, (London,) and that serene, wholesome air, may in all probability expedite my return thither."

To his step-mother he writes:

"Tommy, your first hope, has been some time settled at school, about 25 miles from this place, in a clear wholesome air, & in a family where nothing seems wanting to qualify him as fully to meet your wishes as a school can do. I heard lately from him, & design now & then to pay him a visit, & transmit to you such novelties concerning him as shall occur. This I know will not be disagreeable to that tenderness you express for him, and which I should believe sincere, even tho' I had no other motive than the conformity in your speech and conduct to your dutiful son S. B."

In writing again to his aunts, his father's sisters, he congratulates them on bearing "their late loss" with "such a frame of mind as will enable the person blessed with it

to make the most of the happiness this world affords, by
despising what others would call misfortunes. I own for
my part, that altho' I have not lived quite so long in the
world as yourself, I have yet lived long enough to know,
that there is nothing here worth giving myself one moment's uneasiness about. I therefore doubt not that your
greater experience will induce you to think so too."

These relations having some time afterwards applied to
their nephew Stephen, for pecuniary aid, which the state
of his own affairs at that time made it impossible for him
to render, he writes in their behalf to his rev. great-
uncle, who was also their uncle, to entreat him to transfer
an offer of kindness made previously to himself, to these,
their mutual relations. This well written and interesting
appeal, we find was eventually successful ; but with his
usual impatience, not being satisfied with the slow movements of his rev. uncle, he makes use of a mutual friend
to send him his " duty and hearty thanks," to be accompanied by this remark, " that he who bestows in time, bestows twice"—words worth remembering ! as are also those
with which he closes his farewell letter to his aunts, viz. :
" That health and happiness (the latter of which is still and
always in your own power) may attend you both, is the
hearty prayer of," &c.

In a long letter on politics to his Uncle Hynson, date
London, 1734, he adds : " But since methinks I see you
smile to hear a young man talk of what he is utterly un-
acquainted with, I shall conclude this matter with saying,
that unless a young man discovers his ignorance to those
who are able to inform him, 'tis unlikely he should ever
know anything."

It appears openly at last, that the beautiful Miss Peggy Shippen was the object of his admiration! Whilst in London he receives the account of her being engaged, and afterwards of her being married to a gentleman of Boston. He expresses the most earnest wishes for her happiness, and endeavors to show some magnanimity towards the object of her choice, which is, however, accompanied by some of his satirical touches—perhaps those who have ever been deeply in love, may be able to excuse him!

His rev. great-uncle having expressed a desire to understand the state of his affairs with the Lord Baltimore, he writes him a long letter of explanation, from which we will give some extracts:

" 'Tis a dispute between the Ld. Baltimore and myself arising upon an endeavor of his to vacate his own grant given to my Father and another person for the quantity of 230 acres of land, each of which is worth at least £100 sterlg."—" My father has by his Will, among other things, divided his share thereof amongst us his children : there is in such part as comes to me a very beautiful hill* (and it is mentioned in his Will): With this spot his Lordship during the time of his being in Maryland professed to be greatly enamoured, & at last determined to do his utmost towards getting the same into his possession, under pretence of building a Governor's house thereon."

" And as the metropolis of that province is built only on the said 230 acres, if his Ldship can by this method vacate that grant, he has besides the forementioned advantages, the fee-simple of the whole town in himself, and will

* The hill in the center of the city, on which the State-house was afterwards built.

4

then either oblige the respective inhabitants to re-purchase at a full value, or else to pay a very considerable annual rent—a very considerable improvement of his revenue, and another, indeed a main reason for his present conduct ; for the hope of gaining more is always the main spring of action to an avaricious disposition.

" You'll naturally reflect how likely his Ldship's Province is to flourish under his Ldship's oppression !

" . . . . since this is a matter not only of greatest import- ance to myself but likewise to all the private proprietors of the Province, I know not whether I shall not come over again (to England) with it myself—for could I, tho' with the ruin of my whole fortune, baulk his avaricious maw of this morsel of land, and the dangerous precedent, I should glory in the action." " I have many reasons to think that his Ldship has not laid aside his old animosity to *our family*, on account of the many oppositions it has given him in his former endeavors to oppress the people— and least I should follow so good an example as my worthy Father lately left me, of a humane and publick spirit, and knowing that

> Haud facilè emergent quod virtutibus obstat
> Res angusta domi . . . .

he is determined to crush me (in our Court language) and put it out of my power to give them any future oppo- sition." . . . .

In April, 1735, he again leaves England—and his sub- sequent letters to his friends there, show him anxiously supporting his cause against his powerful adversary. He is astonished, on returning to Maryland, to find the pro- gress things have made in the province, during the short interval of a year, "towards an absolute and despotick government;" and although his interest in that affair is the interest of the whole people, he fears they are become so " mean and subservient to the Court party" that they will " rather see him utterly ruined in this spirited attempt, than help him to success by their timely aid."

Notwithstanding his close attention to business, of various descriptions, he never omits writing to his absent friends, both in England and America; and knowing the fact of his having an immense run of business as a lawyer, besides his fondness for social life, we might be surprised at his voluntarily accomplishing these epistolary tasks, did we not reflect on the power and beauty of order, system, and punctuality, which have the effect of creating time for all things, and developing new resources.

To his brother Tom, left at school in England, he writes long and very interesting letters, conveying information and advice suitable to his age, and which, being pleasingly adapted to his capacity and situation, could hardly fail to produce good effects on his mind—or indeed on that of any one who peruses them thoughtfully.

To Mr. Harris, Speaker of the House of Assembly, who was connected with the family both by birth and marriage, he writes long familiar letters, sometimes on politics, paper currency, &c. To give some idea of his drollery and humor we will extract a passage from one of these, where, after having written five closely-filled pages on the above subjects, he abruptly says : " But hang politicks ! and since I am somewhat ashamed of breaking off before my letter be run to a moderate length, let us return to our jocose conversation. If my particular friend's vehicle had but

four wheels, tho' it were as little as a wheelbarrow, methinks I could look very big in it, but I cannot endure the
thoughts of riding in a sledge, like one going to the gal-
lows ;—I will therefore choose to wait till she procures
herself a Coach, & I doubt not but my patience will be
well repaid by the satisfaction I shall have in reflecting on
the two pretty figures we shall make in it," &c.

His half-sister, Miss Frisby, having informed him of
some ill-natured remark which had been made against
him, he replies with that sportive indifference and composure which marks true self-respect on these occasions, and
recommending her to be quite easy, he adds : " I do not
find that it (the report) at all infringes on my liberty &
gaiety ; for it is with me now, as it used to be, every day
is holiday with me."

Yet, notwithstanding his fine animal spirits, his energy
of character, and his firm standing in society, we find, in
a letter to an intimate friend in England, dated Annapolis,
September, 1736, the following confession : " I am still
in an unsettled condition ; as not being certain whether I
shall ever be able to speak in public ; having several times
attempted it with the utmost agony and confusion to myself; and what is worst of all, without any signs of its
becoming more easy and familiar to me.   I am determined
once more to make tryal, and if I fail of success, I think I
must of necessity give it over :—how I may dispose of
myself afterwards, I am not yet determined."   This
occurred several years after he had been admitted to practice, and should be remembered by all those young lawyers
who may chance to have similar difficulties in their own
feelings ; for Mr. Bordley not only overcame them by per-

severing endeavors, but he soon afterwards became a distinguished lawyer, was thronged with great practice, and maintained his professional standing to the close of his life.

As to his suit with Lord Baltimore, it was decreed against him in the Maryland Courts, and he transferred it by appeal to England. At one time it seemed to prosper, but some difficulty afterwards occurred that appears to have delayed the settlement of it to a later period.

In the mean while, he was very comfortably settled at Annapolis, in the rising practice of his profession, and in the easy and truly social enjoyment of good society, for which he had a decided propensity; and perhaps few old bachelors so well understood doing the honors of his own house—for his leading principle was, an open-hearted hospitality to those he believed deserving. He had invited his only sister to keep house for him; and in their mutual affection and respect, their sensible and moderate views of life, and the respectful regard of their numerous connections and acquaintances, they appear to have possessed, and to have been sensible of the possession, as much happiness as usually falls to the lot of mortals. The following family sketch, from a letter to his aunts, Mary and Elizabeth Bordley, in England, will show his warm affections as a brother, and also his predilection for a rural life, which we believe to have been sincere, notwithstanding the evidence of his conduct to the contrary. Many are those mortals, thronging together in a city, whose career exhibits this apparent inconsistency, but in fact their beautiful consistency in the course of duty. Nature gives to all her children this fondness for the scenes of her

4*

domain—education and circumstances enable them often
to act on some principle of duty opposed to it.

"In compliance with your request, I must inform you of
the situation of our family : I have two own Brothers &
one Sister; the eldest is my brother Will, who has now
been of age some time & is very capable of doing for himself in that kind of life which in my opinion is by far the
most happy; I mean that of a Planter;* it affording a
good income, & being destitute of the noise & bustle &
stir which attends those who are obliged to lead their
lives amongst great numbers of people; and whose liveli-
hood of course depends upon the smiles of those who, from
the nature of their employment, are often inclined to
frown; whilst the honest peaceable labour & industry of
the other, procures him a sweet & pleasant & independent
repose, affording him not only a certain means of living,
but likewise of living well. My Brother Johnny is now
about 16 & still at school here, intending for the same
kind of employment with his Brother Will.—My sister
Bett is between 19 & 20—and is one for whose sake alone
I could choose to live, and should have but little inclination to continue here after the happening of anything to
deprive me of her; or to lessen that affection which I now
bear her; and which I think I ought, so long as she con-
tinues to do nothing whereby she may forfeit it. She is
still single, and in my opinion, since she has a fortune
independent of any one, she will be best off while she con-
tinues so; tho' I would not be understood as if I was
against her marrying if she were so inclined; but only to

* "Planter" was then synonymous with husbandman, or one who lived by
cultivating his estate, and living on it.

let you see that I think there are so few men who may be
trusted with the happiness of a woman of education or
delicacy, that the hazard is not worth running; and of this
she is herself sensible; indeed there are very few to whom
I could trust her's. I am likewise still single; and at
present continue so as well to avoid the noise and uneasiness of a large family & the continual labour and fatigue
of providing fortunes to be left them at my death, as the
lessening my power of doing for my dear Bett anything
that may contribute towards making her happy. I have
also three half Brothers, Thomas, Matthias, and Beale;
the eldest of whom is now in England, under Mr. Saml.
Hyde's care, Merchant in London—to whom any letters
may be sent; the other two are at school here. Since my
Father's death, his wife has married again, and they have
had three sons and one daughter; the eldest and the
youngest were both boys and are both dead. Before she
married my Father, she had three girls by a former husband, all now living, the eldest and the youngest married
off. So when we are all together, we can almost make
enough to carry a Borough Election, allowing us all votes.
Annapolis, Sept., 1737."

His correspondence with young Mr. M. Harris, of some
years' standing, is quite voluminous, including a variety
of topics, discussed between them in an interesting way:
religion, government, literature, friendship, courtship,
manners, &c., each take their turn; and though treated in
that frank and ingenuous way that is so becoming in a
familiar correspondence, they nevertheless convey many
solid and valuable reflections and opinions, without either
ostentation or bigotry. The young friend seeks, by means

of inquiry, to be enlightened by the other's experience and knowledge; the senior meets these researches with the overflowing abundance of his own good humor and mental wealth; and when we consider the superior acquired advantages of his mind, as well as its native acuteness and sagacity, we cannot but congratulate that young gentleman on having obtained the willing assistance of such a friend.

> " The friend thou hast, and his adoption tried,
> Grapple him to thy soul with hooks of steel."

But we are grieved to be obliged to acknowledge that the blessing was not sufficiently estimated. Pride, alas! false pride, stepped in between the young man and his best interests! Perhaps he was afraid, being the younger, of acknowledging himself inferior; that fear, which proves the existence of real inferiority! Perhaps he thought, as unhappily too many do, that putting on a bold aspect would conceal the truth—not reflecting that Truth, the sacred emanation from the light of Heaven, can never be concealed.

The youth appears to have fought hard to reject the improvement within his reach, by caviling at trifles, playing off flashes of false wit and unmeaning repartee, and at last venturing, with equal ingratitude and folly, to assail the motives of his enlightened friend.

Then it is, that Stephen's amiable character shines forth. For a long while, and letter after letter, he gently parries the other's unkind thrusts, takes the trouble to point out his misapprehensions, and by alternate drollery and remonstrance to set the other right respecting his friendship—which was in fact the only motive that could actuate him in a private correspondence with a young person, residing far from him, and possessing neither the power to promote or to interfere with his interests in any way whatever. At last, finding it impossible to make a blind man see, he determines to stop the correspondence; he withholds an answer, already written, (seven pages of kind and forcible explanation,) and confines himself to sending a few lines on some pretended business, without noticing the other's impertinence. The ultimate consequence was, that the tyro received no more improving speculations—he was not reproached—he was not quite deserted—the generosity of his friend still endured, and smiled at his weakness—but he had checked its gay and genial flow; that first fine glow of the heart, which, once chilled, can never beam again with the same warmth!

Alas! how common are such mistakes in young people— and also, in some who never come to years of wisdom! Too many of us, of all ages, avoid looking to the consequences of our own conduct. It requires a good player, either at chess, or in the game of life, to see several moves ahead! Yet He, who gives us the noble faculty of reason, also requires us to use it—and, let us never forget, that He will also require us to give an account of it to Him!

In 1750, Mr. Bordley gives the following little family views to one of his relations in the north of England:

"We live well, and cheerfully, with the enjoyment of all the necessaries and many of the little comforts of life. I wish we could, without inconvenience to yourselves, have your whole family, big & little, by our fireside the ensuing Christmas." * * * * "We are all still single; a strange family! perhaps you'll say; but Beale is now in pursuit of a Dove, and I am apt to believe will soon break the enchantment."

"My next Brother is William, who lives on his own land, which is of the best sort amongst us, & as good as any in England; and is one whom you would call a Gentleman-farmer. The next is John, a trader—these are our own Brothers. The following are by a different mother: Matthias, who has a genteel and beneficial place under Government; and Beale, who now and for several years past has lived with me, is a trader."* "Amidst a great plenty of everything, we enjoy as fine and serene an air as any in the world—our winter is generally sharp, but dry; and our summer warm, but healthy."

In the manner of life already slightly described, Stephen Bordley continued to pass his years in uninterrupted quiet and satisfaction; enjoying a goodly portion of the comforts and luxuries that he best liked; and sharing them largely and liberally with his relations, friends, and acquaintances. His house was headquarters to his kindred of every degree; and he appears to have been dissatisfied with his brothers' visits, if they did not bring their wives and children with them—and shows in his family letters an amiable interest in all their little concerns.

His intimates were the Tilghmans, as before mentioned; the Dulanys, Carrolls, &c., including all the first society of Annapolis, amongst whom he was a great favorite—and no wonder! for he delighted to promote gayety amongst the young, and was seconded by his sister in giving them frequent entertainments; and particularly in keeping a

* This was written at the time that Beale had renounced the law to try commerce, which, not liking, he afterwards resumed the law.

good table, every day hospitably ready. If there was one article in which he was more luxurious than another, it was in wines: these he prided himself in having of the best, and in abundance. In his orders to the celebrated house of Hill & Co., for a pipe of Madeira, he says: "A pipe of your best Madeira wine, cost what it will; as I do not stint you in price, I hope you will not slight me in the wine." We find in his orders, bills, &c. repeated items of this kind: "A Cask of Champagne, and two of Burgundy," addressed to his regular French merchants. In his familiar letter, is now and then a hint to some particular friend, that he reserves a "few dozen of Burgundy for him;" as for instance, to his favorite, James Tilghman, he says: "My Burgundy is almost out; but I shall keep some of that as well as of Champagne till the Provincial Court, when I hope we shall share it together." In all this, there was a gentlemanly liberality without extravagance; for no one could be more exact in regulating his expenses according to his means, and squaring his inclination by his ability. The remarkable and neat regularity of his accounts, exemplary even now to behold! prove the justice of this remark—and he says himself, when recommending this habit of keeping exact accounts, to an intimate friend: "I know by this method every article coming in and going out; and particularly I find that my housekeeping costs me in 1750 ******, which gives me a plain hint to live more frugally. This method takes some time, but is fully compensated by knowing every article of charge, and at the year's end what one is worth to a farthing!"

He was a man who delighted to be liberal and generous, and to promote others' comforts was his joy; but he would never be imposed on. Nature had provided him with a weapon of defense as powerful when well managed, as any other; and this was a satirical humor, and a pointed wit, that evidently kept his enemies in awe. He used it most freely in the course of some political conflicts in which he was engaged; and there is a pamphlet now by us, which strongly marks his talent in wielding it. To his friends, who were numerous, it was playful and harmless humor, and proved that the fancy which used it was completely under the control of the possessor. This worthy old bachelor, for such he remained, was a great favorite amongst the ladies of the first circle of Annapolis, where his society and conversation were much sought after—they smiled at his primitive and precise politeness, but justly admired his wit, good sense, and good humor. His satirical vein was felt only by his assailants, but woe to those who induced him to draw an arrow in self-defense!

He resided in the old family house, on taking possession of which, he sent to England for complete suits of household furniture, plate, &c. Its noblest furniture, however, was an extensive law and miscellaneous library, amply stocked with the best editions of well-selected works, in various languages, to which he was constantly adding, and, reading as he added—his opinions, showing a good critical taste of the different authors and subjects of the day, are largely expressed in some of his familiar letters; he seems always to have read to good purpose; and neither law nor politics could conquer his favorite pursuit of general knowledge.

As a lawyer, he stood high; and though surrounded in that day by able competitors, his practice was very extensive. His close application, steadiness, order, and punctuality, were proverbially marked and admired. He was for some time high in influence in the General Assembly of Maryland, and held several valuable offices under the Provincial Government. Coming, at twenty-one, into possession of a considerable patrimonial estate, successful in law practice, and holding various lucrative appointments, he amassed a handsome property; with which he lived liberally to the extent of his income, and contributed largely to the enjoyment of others, without squandering his means. There seemed nothing wanting to his happiness but a wife! Like many of his brotherhood, he was an admirer of the fair sex, and fond of being rallied for his admiration of handsome individuals amongst them—though we believe he was only once in sober earnest on this subject. He acquired some quaint old bachelor peculiarities; amongst them was the virtue of neatness carried rather to an extreme precision, in everything under his direction, from the arrangement of his books and papers down to the minutest attentions of the toilette. To this day this neatness is evident in his voluminous files of papers, and in his many and exact account books, copies of orders to his distant merchants,* letter books, files of letters, &c.

He delighted in manly sports. There is a letter from him to a young friend, accompanying the present of a valuable bow and arrows, made of the yew-tree, in which he gives directions with characteristic minuteness and precision, both for the manner of using it, and of keeping it when out of use. He seems, indeed, to have been never

---

* In these are some now curious articles, as " Two black wigs," " Two pieces of the *finest* Holland linen," " Three ditto of the best Cambrick," &c.

5

happier than when contributing to the amusement or instruction of young persons.

He enjoyed a robust constitution and general health till
within a short time of his death, which took place Dec. 6,
1764, at his own house, in Annapolis. We cannot give
a better account of this event than from the pen of his
brother Beale, in a letter to a relation and friend, viz.:

"The flattering hopes we had of my Brother's being re-
lieved of his Palsy, vanished very suddenly—but a week
before his death, which was on the 6th Ins^t he thought
himself so well as to wish to follow me up to Baltimore—
yet for the most part he had for many months before been
assured within himself that he could not recover, of which
he often told me, and seemed rather desirous of death than
otherwise. No one ever died more composed and even
cheerfully resigned—he was placid from the moment he
quitted the thoughts of all business, which was about two
months before the fatal moment—he gradually wasted
away, (the effects of the Palsy,) and died in my arms on
his Couch, without a groan, being sensible of the approach,
and of everything about him, two minutes before. I had
got to him about three hours before. Near the beginning
of his Will, he blesses God for the many mercies vouch-
safed to him thro' the course of this mortal life, and for
the prospect of a happy Eternity thro' the sufferings, death
and resurrection of our blessed Saviour Jesus Christ; and
towards the end he concludes—'In witness whereof (with
the highest sense of gratitude and most fervent thanks to
Almighty God for his many undeserved blessings), &c.'
He was always unaffectedly religious, and his many notes
and readings on the subject shew it, even from the time

he was at school—but he always modestly disapproved of
the trappings and outside, taking the greatest pains to
improve and elevate his mind with a reverence and respect
for the Deity—He did not doubt of the truths of the Christian Religion. But I cannot omit mentioning a text which
he wrote in large letters at the beginning of one of his
note-books on this subject—'Where mystery begins, there
Religion ends.' For my part I have always looked on it
that Religion, (the Christian Religion,) so far as at this
time is necessary for us to know, is simple, pure, and un-
compounded."

He bequeathed his library with his whole estate to his
only remaining brother, Beale; subject to an annuity, with
the use of his house, furniture, &c., to his sister—and leaving several legacies of (£1000) one thousand pounds each
to some other relations.

WILLIAM BORDLEY

Was the second son of Thomas and Rachel Bordley. He
was born at Annapolis in 1716. He was educated in England as before mentioned, with his brother Stephen, and
intended for a mercantile profession, but after a short
trial of this business he relinquished it and returned home,
where on coming of age, he settled on a farm in Cecil
County, Maryland. There he held several profitable offices,
and maintained a respectable plain character. He resided
principally on his estate until his death, which took place
in 1762. He married a Miss Pearce, and left a son and
daughter, who both died in infancy.

ELIZABETH BORDLEY

Was the third child of Thomas and Rachel Bordley, and the only daughter. She was born in 1717, in the old family house at Annapolis. In that city she principally passed her life amid the social gayeties of its distinguished society, residing with her brother Stephen during his life, and afterwards in the same mansion, which was bequeathed to her for life by him. After the death of that brother, she passed most of her summers at Wye Island, with her only remaining brother, Beale, to whom she was much attached.

In her youth she was considered handsome and was much admired. Her conduct through life obtained for her the highest respect, and she was greatly beloved for the gentleness and benevolence of her disposition. Several eligible offers of marriage were made to her, but she was never persuaded to marry. When young, she had given the first affection of her heart to an amiable and exemplary young man, who died in England, and though she " never told her love," this was generally understood to be the cause of her remaining single. After her death, some verses and other tender tokens from her parting lover were found still faithfully preserved in a pocket-book, which had been scrupulously concealed from common view. This fond fidelity did not at all depress her mind, or cloud her brow ; she was remarkable for being always serene and cheerful, temperate in all her habits, diffident of herself, pleased with social life and its innocent amuse-ments, and contributing always her full share towards pro-moting the gayety and happiness of young persons.

Something of this amiable part of her character may be ascribed to natural constitution, and we cannot, at this day, pretend to estimate the proportion of self-conquering merit which was hers; but she was born with quick feelings, and too great sensibility for her own happiness, and we may therefore, without hesitation, ascribe great part of the harmony and suavity of her conduct as well as manners, to the simple and beautiful fact, that she was throughout life, sincerely, unaffectedly and unassumingly religious; in her youth, a dutiful daughter of the Protestant Episcopal Church, in her latter years, clinging to the hopes and comforts which that early and devout attention to the subject had opened to her view. Then, in the evening of the long protracted day, when the sunshine of this world's charms had set, and left only the bright glow of remembrance behind, then was her previously obedient spirit made happy in its anticipations. The writer remembers well the effect of this inward treasure on her always cheerful mind, and the private comfort she derived from the constant companion of her retired hours, her Bible, whose blessed precepts and joyous tidings, she endeavored to lay before those young minds connected with her, while in herself, she was ever ready to prove their power by kindness and sympathy to all within her circle of influence; and let it be remembered, that such a character never loses its influence. However modest, however small, its work is sure, "for it is founded upon a rock," " the rock of ages."

She had naturally a good understanding, and when her strength of mind was put to the test, she could evince a steady firmness, not always found in union with such a

gentle disposition.   If some few prejudices were occasionally found tarnishing such merit, the fault might be ascribed more to the state of opinion in those around her,
and to the general ignorance of the times than to herself;
but they were never violent or vindictive, or injurious in
their effects on others, and when they were borne patiently,
her mind has been led to see and to correct some of those
errors of opinion, and she had then the triumph of showing that magnanimity which can acknowledge a mistake.

She was delicately formed, yet of sound and healthful
constitution, temperate and neat in all her habits, ladylike
and easy in her manners, unaffected, and obtaining respect
for herself by her good treatment of others.   She was
fond of substantial attire, and always adhered to the fashion that grew up with her, of rich silks and brocades, lace
ruffles, &c.   One of her nieces has a portrait of her, painted
by C. W. Peale, which gives a tolerably faithful likeness of
her when turned of middle age.

A few months before her death, she was attacked, like
her brother Stephen, with a paralytic affection, which after
two or three returns, terminated her life on the 28th Nov.,
1789, in her 73d year.

She had been prepared by the duteous habits of her life
for this event, and saw its approach with a Christian's
tranquillity.   She had banished from her mind the last
worldly care, by making her will, and all other temporal
arrangements some time previous to the last attack of the
fatal disease.   She left her only brother, Beale, principal
heir to her estate, remembering several other relatives in
handsome legacies, and provided amply for her old family
domestics.

JOHN BORDLEY

Was the fourth child and third son of Thomas and Rachel Bordley. He was born at Annapolis in 1721. He married young, and settled on the Eastern Shore of Maryland, near to Chestertown. He died in 1761, leaving no child. Nothing more is known to the writer of the incidents of his life.

THOMAS BORDLEY

Was the first child of the above-mentioned Thomas Bordley and Ariana, his wife, (intermarried as before stated in 1723.) He was born at Annapolis in 1724, and when ten years old accompanied his step-father, Mr. Jenings, and his half-brother, Stephen, to England, where they established and left him for a course of education. When that object was completed, he immediately entered on the study of law, and continued that pursuit until admitted to practice. He was a youth of uncommon promise, and early evinced an unusual degree of excellence both in intellectual and moral qualities. His letters, some of which are still existing, to his family, when only sixteen, are, for that age, models, not only for good composition, and good penmanship, but also for the infinitely higher possessions of good sense, affection, and sincerity. His handwriting also had a characteristic beauty; it was strong, clear, and graceful. His conduct and behavior harmonized with

these exemplifications of excellence, and won all who knew,
to love him.

After being twelve years in England, he revisited his
native country in 1746, but it had lost the attractions of a
home to him, and he remained only about six months,
long enough to delight his relatives and fix their affections
on such evident and high merit, but not long enough to
change his views, which were decidedly for practicing the
law in England. To that country he returned; soon afterwards took the small-pox and died of it at the early
age of twenty-three, in 1747.

MATTHIAS BORDLEY,

Second son of Thomas and Ariana Bordley, was born at
Annapolis in 1725; there he was also educated. He early
settled as a planter and tobacco merchant in Harford
County, Maryland, and held a lucrative and respectable
office under the Provincial Government. He married Miss
Peggy Bigger, when she was just sixteen, very pretty,
well educated, and amiable, and he was devotedly attached to her. Their affection was mutual and pure; the
writer of this has often heard his youngest brother, Beale,
speak of them emphatically as an instance of strong genuine affection and connubial happiness in two equally amiable beings. But, alas! it was not to endure long; she died in
giving birth to her first child, and he never recovered from
the shock, but, after lingering a few months in a state of

fixed and unyielding grief, he followed her to the grave in the year 1756, aged thirty-one.

They were considered a very interesting young couple, their affection had been the theme of much admiration, and caused a deeper tone of feeling for their loss, which was long deplored. The lines on "Theodosius and Constantia" were often applied to them :

> " They were lovely in their lives,
> And in their deaths they were not divided."

END OF PART FIRST.

BIOGRAPHICAL SKETCHES

OF THE

BORDLEY FAMILY,

OF MARYLAND, &c.

PART SECOND.

A FAMILIAR SKETCH

OF THE

LIFE AND CHARACTER

OF

JOHN BEALE BORDLEY.

—

Dedicated Affectionately

TO HIS

CHILDREN AND GRANDCHILDREN,

BY

THEIR NEAR RELATIVE AND FAITHFUL FRIEND,

THE AUTHOR.

Philadelphia, 1826.

6

GENTLE READER.

—

BEFORE entering on the following attempt at a memoir, accept the writer's acknowledgment of its many and great deficiencies, and pause one moment, whilst we point out and explain some of them.

Of the entire first half of the life here sketched, the writer had no personal knowledge, and no means of collecting much concerning it from others living in the present day. The respected individual himself was not in the habit of bringing it into view, in later periods, being otherwise engaged, and, moreover, as remarkable for the absence of egotism and ostentation in his family communications, as in those less private. So that even his older children knew little of his prime of life, except what occurred within their own actual observation, which also was limited by their long residences from home in pursuit of education.

Thus it happens that we have been compelled to leave those parts of our sketch most in shade, which would probably have yielded the most gratifying variety of incidents, could their minute traces have come to light.

The few prominent points of that earlier portion of his

career, which are here preserved, have been gathered from old family records, such as letters, accounts, note-books, &c., and from traditional recollections confirmed by a few yet living evidences.

Pains have been taken throughout to set down nothing, either in this or the preceding outlines of lives, but what the writer on sound grounds believes to be true, and can prove to rest on good authority. For the accuracy of the narrative, as far as relates to the latter years of the life now inscribed to you, she is herself a living voucher.

Accept it, ye of the same blood, even " with all its im-perfections on its head," accept it as a test of good-will, or, as a hint of what might have been done, had the mate-rials and the pen been equal to the subject.

Remember the writer, only as your faithful relative, and now receive, clothed with a sister Christian's hopes, her affectionate farewell.   E. B. G.

PHILADELPHIA, Walnut Street.

December, 1826.

BIOGRAPHICAL SKETCHES, &c.

JOHN BEALE BORDLEY,

Son of the Thomas and Ariana Bordley before mentioned, was born at Annapolis, Maryland, on the 1st of February, 1727, O. S., (the 11th February, new style,) four months after his father's death. He was thus a posthumous child, and the youngest of his father's seven children.

He received no uncommon advantages of education early in life, but he afterwards acquired, by the energy and application of his own mind, all that untoward early circumstances had denied him. His mother being still in the prime of life, and a remarkbly fine woman, was again sought in marriage, and gave her hand to Mr. Edmund Jenings, of Annapolis, her third husband. Though an estimable man, he was hardly equal to the heavy charge of minutely conducting the fortunes and the education of so many step-children—ten, besides his own five; and engaged as he was in public duties and political affairs, their interests rather languished. Yet so amiable and honorable was he, that they were all much attached to him, and never took any measures, or made any remarks to his disadvantage, but lived, as may be seen in Stephen Bordley's letters, like one happy and harmonious family, of the same views and interests; and of this period, the subject of our present sketch had, late in life, a perfect recollection, and

6*

often spoke with animation of the happy family circle over which his mother presided so charmingly, and of the amiable disposition of his step-father.

In 1737, Mrs. Jenings accompanied her husband to England, where, as elsewhere mentioned, she soon afterwards died ; but before leaving America, she placed her son Beale, then 10 years old, under the care of Col. Hynson, of Chestertown, Maryland, and his wife, her sister Francina. There he went through a common school education. His teacher was a worthy man of the name of Peale,* who, perceiving an excellent capacity and uncommon desire of knowledge in young Bordley, prolonged the hours of instruction as far as his abilities extended, by private lessons, and judicious encouragement. This benevolent interest was not bestowed on an ungrateful heart ; it led to that friendship which Mr. Bordley through life showed to the son of his old schoolmaster.

He was remarkable in his youth for an extreme modesty and diffidence, and often in later life, remarked upon it as having been a painful feeling to himself, but as having also proved a happy safeguard to moral principle, which he explained by adding that " the habit of doubting one's self, leads to self-examination, and its good consequences, improvement to ourselves, with justice and forbearance towards others." In this he did not include that false shame, or rather sheepishness, so apt to fasten on badly educated youth, and under which may lurk and hide some of the very worst propensities of the human character, with less chance of their being corrected than if boldly thrown

---

* Father to him, who, in Philadelphia, has identified himself with one of the best museums of Natural History ever established by individual exertion.

open to view; he commended only that true modesty, which
is often seen in the noblest characters, and connected with
the finest talents. Witness Washington and Sir Isaac New-
ton. This modesty has been somewhere defined to be,
" That spirit of discernment which leads a man to understand himself, and to distinguish at a glance the proprie-
ties or improprieties, the merits or demerits, which he ob-
serves in his associates, neither derogating from their
merit, nor arrogating an undue share to himself." It
thus implies an improved judgment, and stands in direct
opposition to blundering ignorance and unenlightened pride,
from both which sheepishness arises. It may also be considered in some constitutions, a sensibility to justice, and
a willingness to see the truth, in which case it evinces
moral courage, is accompanied by ingenuous candor, and
often attends the strongest minds in every stage of life,
and in this view, it may be said to have belonged to John
Beale Bordley. But let us return to our narrative.

When Beale was about 17 years of age, his eldest brother
Stephen, returned again from England, having completed
there a nine years' course of law-study under such advantages, that he was at once received into that practice of
the law in Annapolis, for which he was afterwards distinguished. One of his first steps on establishing himself in his
office, was to invite his brother Beale, whom he had never
yet seen, to come and study with him, and adopt the same
profession. In this plan Beale acquiesced gladly, and became a diligent student, both in the law and in general
literature and science, for which reason his studies were
protracted several years beyond the usual period. On his
first introduction to the office, an incident occurred which

had nearly daunted his courage for the undertaking.
When he entered, Stephen threw open the doors of his
extensive miscellaneous and law library, and in his jocose
and humorous way, with which the other was not yet acquainted, said to him : "There, Beale, when you have read
through all those books, you may then practice the law."
An appalling sentence, which, spoken in a serious manner,
was taken seriously, and not easily forgotten. And the
diffidence of youth in the presence, for the first time, of
one so much his senior, (there was 18 years between these
brothers,) preventing any request for explanation, the impression remained, and continued silently and oppressively
operating on the mind of the young student until a decided disgust was formed there against the law. It certainly evinced an uncommon steadiness of character and
self-command, that under these circumstances, he pursued
the study, and even longer than the usual term, giving his
teacher reason to be satisfied with his application and pro-
ficiency. At the same time he completed a course of the
most valuable general reading, laying in an ample stock of
history, philosophy, science, and arts. He has often been
heard by the writer to say, that he felt the benefit of this
course of reading throughout his life, not only for the
actual and useful information gained, but also for the habit
of giving system and stability to thought, and for all this,
he blessed the quiet and the regularity of his brother's
office, the bustle and cares of the world having never afterwards allowed him such a "golden opportunity" for the
acquisition of knowledge.

After an honorable admission to the bar, being still
young and not yet quite in humor with the law, he tried

other pursuits ; made some acquaintance with commerce, as we see by some remarkably neat account books, but liked it still less than the law, and finally gave it up. He did not, however, suffer it to be lost time, and always afterwards congratulated himself on the knowledge of book-keeping which he then acquired, and also the insight into men's professional characters which he gained.

Throughout life, he was fond of particular branches of mathematics: geometrical problems, algebraical and arithmetical calculations, &c. were among his favorite amusements. Surveying was also an agreeable pastime to him ; he sent to England for a very complete surveying apparatus, and amused himself and his friends, by invented opportunities for applying it, which he used to say contributed to keep him in health by the excitement and exercise ; he also observed latterly, that in the course of his life he had sometimes found it a useful branch of knowledge.

It is not known to us when he acquired the Latin language, but he was well acquainted with it, and it was probably one of his studies in his brother's office. In fact, to those who knew him intimately, it was evident that he had not suffered himself to lose time, but that through life he had been in the constant habit of gaining useful knowledge, and this not as an effort, not as a labor that required the stimulus of rivalship or ambition, to give it vigor, nor yet for purposes of ostentation ; it was the easy and pleasant result of an early imbibed principle of conduct, or perhaps it would be most correct to say, the native and strong impulse of his mind, directed by some early impression to a good object, and confirmed and brought into system about the period we are now arrived at.

As familiar letters are said to give an insight into character, it may be interesting to observe how he himself traced the operation of certain reflections on his own conduct by an extract from a letter to a young lawyer, a cousin, dated January, 1765.

" *   *   *   * I have often enjoyed the inward satisfaction arising from acting on fixed principles, disregarding the approbation of the herd. How vain, how weak, how cowardly, to attempt to please all mankind, to overlook the Scriptures with the laws of nature and morality, for the sake of pleasing the vicious or the ignorant multitude by becoming one of them in all measures! Rather let us, firm in good principles, industriously apply to our proper business and not be diverted from a manly employment by the flirting of butterflies. I fortunately (blessed be God) very early, when but a boy, saw the folly of so vain an attempt. I have been ever fixed in a disposition to learn and to do whatever is right without deviating to please others, not but that I am glad to be well with all my neighbors, but never at the expense of counteracting my own rules of action."

Again, still later in life, we find some of the same ideas, in a letter dated 1775, to one of his sons, then at school in England :

" * * * A few principles, early taken up, and closely observed, happily carried me clear of such rocks as many of my cotemporary acquaintances split upon in their youth. Temperance, Resolution to be Myself, against the current of fashion and bent of other youth—choice of sober companions—avoiding idle ones, cards, * * * and wine, and shunning the affectation of being a clever fellow amongst the great or little vulgar, these are great preservatives.

" Go on, my dear Matt, & do well ! I find you have some turn to oratory—improve this ; but let Truth & Justice be the basis of your harangues—feel for the innocent, the injured, and oppressed—it will give a multiplied force to your words—avoid the flowery, diffusive fustian of insincerity, affectation, and vanity," &c.

We have here quoted more than we at first intended ; but we trust that the repetition of such sentiments cannot be unwelcome to any one who, as Cowper says,

" * * * * has a mind, and keeps it."

They serve, besides, to show a marked trait in the character of John Beale Bordley, similar to that which the reader must have observed throughout the sketch of his father's life, as also in his brother's—perhaps we might say it was a Bordley feature ! It seems scarcely necessary to mention it, yet lest there be any misapprehension of our meaning, we will name this family trait, " Independence of Mind."

On attaining his majority, Mr. Bordley came into possession of a pretty patrimonial portion, chiefly in lands, and not very productive, but yielding a snug competence for a young man to begin life with. He was soon, however, so fortunate as to obtain a fair help-mate in the career before him ; in his twenty-fourth year he married Miss Margaret Chew, daughter of Mr. Samuel Chew, of Maryland, and Henrietta Maria his wife, daughter of Mr. and Mrs. —— Dulany.

Miss Chew possessed some fortune from her father,

which afterwards received an addition on the death of her mother.

In the luxurious, pleasant ease of the fashionable society of Annapolis, at that time in its zenith, there was great temptation to a young man, just united to the wife of his choice, who was accustomed to delicacy and refinement, to desire to continue in this fascinating circle of pleasure; but we find that Mr. Bordley, young and ardent as he was, resisted the temptation, and looking forward to future emergencies, retreated in good time to Joppa, a small town on Gunpowder River, between Harford and Baltimore, and in the neighborhood of which lay a large tract of his patrimonial estate.

There he experienced the reward, that sooner or later attends virtuous exertion, and found happiness associated with duty.

With a disposition gay and sprightly—as those who may have heard him describe his joyous feelings at a fox-chase will know how to give him full credit for—he nevertheless very early established a solid reputation for industry and steadiness, as well as for other qualifications; and in 1753, in his twenty-sixth year, he was appointed by the Governor to the office of Prothonotary, or Clerk of Baltimore County, which then included Harford County. This was the most important and most lucrative of any of those clerkships. In the steady pursuance of the duties of this appointment, he resided in and near Joppa between twelve and thirteen years. Here he raised a large family of children, and in their infant attractions and the formation of their opening minds, together with the well-ordered and simple comforts of his rural domicile, always hospitably ready for friends, he found abundant relaxation from the cares of business.

He chose for his fixed residence one of his farms near the town, fitted up a neat house, comfortably established his rising family, and occasionally amused himself with farming. This, to a mind like his, was a happy relief from the irksome business of a county court-house, or even from a prothonotary's office.

It seems probable that here was laid the foundation of that partiality for agriculture and rural affairs which afterwards became his ruling passion, and the solacing amusement of his declining age. Forty years afterwards, when traveling in that direction, he pointed across the country towards Joppa, and said to his youngest daughter: "There, in the neighborhood of that little town, your father passed some of the busiest, and the happiest years of his life. Yes! happy—for there I learned to love Nature!"

And from his papers and account books it appears that even at that early period he was in the practice of sending to England for "the best" farming machines, the best seeds, treatises on husbandry—and among the latter is "Young's Six Weeks' Tour," by which he always set great store.

In 1762, his half-brother William died. In 1765 he wrote thus to his widow's brother, Mr. Pearce: "If your sister is willing, I will put my nephew to school,* and whilst he shall be under my care, will be at the expense of his schooling and board. I am desirous he should have as good an opportunity for education as my own sons."

---

* This kind intention was prevented by the boy's death.

In 1764 he lost his brother Stephen, an event he deeply felt ; and we find him immediately sending to England for a suitable monument, inscription, &c. There had been a steady affection between these brothers, cemented by constant intercourse and interchange of kind offices, and heightened on the part of Beale by a kind of filial respect, Stephen having acted like a father towards him, being eighteen years older, and also the eldest of the family. Soon after this event, Beale writes thus to a mutual friend : " * * * His loss to my sister and myself, who are now the only survivors of my Father's children, is not to be supplied. I know no one so warm, so steady in his friendships and social regards—he was to many here a pattern of virtue, industry, and prudence—but I must stop."*

*   *   *   *   *   *

It was not generally known for some years of his life, that Mr. Bordley's first Christian name was John ; having an elder brother of that name, he omitted the use of it, or only signed with the initial of it, and was called " Beale" only.   After some time, however, he resumed it, and thus mentions the circumstance in a letter to a friend, dated " Annapolis, December 13, 1764."

" You observe I make use of the initial J in signing my name—this has been only since the death of my elder brother John, and for some little time when first of age. I was christened by the name of John Beale, and shall continue to use it for the future."

During his attendance on the courts as Prothonotary, the law and he became so well reconciled, that he seriously

* See the sketch of Stephen's life.

renewed his attention to it, and became a practicing lawyer for several years, with great success, as the writer
remembers to have heard said of him ; and as appears by
his books. His practice was at first, and principally, in
Cecil County, adjoining Harford, and also in the latter,
and in Baltimore County, and was continued with exclusive
attention, when, on relinquishing the office of Prothonotary,
he removed to Baltimore-town, as it was then called.

He was impelled by his own feelings to resign this office,
rather than be answerable under the *Stamp Act*, and the
other " arbitrary and cruel proceedings," as he called
them, of that period. His mind was invariably opposed to
all oppression, and his letters, about that time, are replete
with expressions of natural and indignant feeling on the
unreasonable and injurious treatment of the British government, to which he was amongst the first awakened.
That odious Act was repealed soon after, but he had
already, in 1765, removed to Baltimore. There he was
comfortably settled in that improving town, and continued
the practice of the law with the most flattering prospects.

These, however, he was induced to relinquish ; for in
1766 he was appointed one of the Judges of the Provincial
Court, for Maryland. These courts were held twice a
year, at Annapolis, the seat of government ; and their
jurisdiction required many circuits, and gave their Judges
frequent intercourse with the eastern as well as western
shore of the Chesapeake. In 1767 he also received the
appointment of Judge of the Admiralty.* He held both

* On the death of the Chief Justice Hooper, in 1767, Governor Eden offered
the vacant chair to Judge Bordley, but he declined it, and as we see by a memorandum in his note-book, recommended Mr. Hayward, who was afterwards
appointed to it.

these judicial offices until the change of Government in
1776.

Persons are yet living, who remember the character of
high respectability which he sustained upon the bench,
and also the decorum and tranquillity maintained in the
courts where he presided. He was an admirer and a supporter of good order, which he considered as the necessary
safeguard to property, but it was held in his mind as being
always subservient to the cause of justice and mercy. He
viewed it as one of the appointed means, under Providence, by which society in a civilized and Christian state
is held together, for the promotion of higher objects. He
was remarkable for attention to the interests of all who
were oppressed, and for strict adherence to principle, of
which he permitted no evasion, either in great or in small
affairs. As an instance of the latter, it has been mentioned that having sometimes observed lawyers endeavoring to intimidate young and ignorant witnesses, either for
their amusement or the benefit of their cause, he set about
and soon accomplished a complete reform in the manners of
the bar—gave courage and support to embarrassed witnesses, and taught the examining counsel a better regard
for his own dignity.

The late Judge Breckenridge, of Pennsylvania, mentioned, some few years since, the pleasure he used to take,
when a lad, in attending the courts where Judge Bordley
presided. He related various circumstances, and some
anecdotes, which had struck his attention, of which only
one is now within our reach—but we will mention it just
as related to Mr. Bordley's eldest daughter, and by her to
the writer : A celebrated young lawyer of that day, Mr.

Samuel C——, was pleading for a client who was accused and prosecuted, by a tanner, for stealing a calf's skin, and he was eloquently and satirically endeavoring to acquit him, on the ground that it was too trifling to be considered a theft. Judge Bordley fixed his eyes calmly on the lawyer, and in his own pleasant, attractive and peculiarly impressive manner, said : "Ah! Mr. C——, is it you who think that, because the article is of small value, there is no theft?" The lawyer hung his head and said no more! Judge Breckenridge then added: "I do not remember how the cause ended, but I never can forget the Judge's manner! nor the deep feeling of sound principle conveyed by it from his mind to my own!"

In matters of importance he was a firm, and was called a strict Judge. Doubtless he was so; but it was for the accuracy of the general result, not for any particular point gained; while by all it has been admitted, that the native goodness of his heart, and the frank generosity of his temper, kept those around him happy and harmonious.

It was his well known and well appreciated love of justice, and his unequivocal support of truth, which gave him a weight of character and an influence that he never claimed for himself, by any personal, extraneous, or even official rights. His highest ambition was to be the organ or the engine for administering to the rights of others, and for awakening, from the bench, an enlightened and general sense of justice and propriety.

This unaffected source of dignity, this clear moral perception, sustained by a sound sense of religion and respect for the laws, was the more readily felt, acknowledged, and respected, because it did not infringe on the easy, genuine

7*

urbanity and playfulness of manner, which were also and equally his striking characteristics. He had no mock dignity, yet he could be serious. In one of his note-books there is a sketch of one of his charges to the jury, in which we trace his own vigorous mode of reasoning on general views, set forth in the simplest language, breathing throughout a solemn sense of responsibility to the Great Judge of all, and a brotherly feeling in explaining the duties of those he addressed.

But neither his public and private duties, nor the charms of good society, in which he delighted, and shared abundantly at Annapolis, could enfeeble his warm parental interest; the education of his children was to him an object of primary concern; and we find by many letters on the subject, that after various investigation of the public schools in our own country, he addressed the following anxious inquiries respecting the education of his sons, to his half-brother, Mr. Edmund Jenings, in London, 1766:

"* * * The most weighty charge on my mind at present, and the most difficult, is procuring a right education for my children. A good school for useful learning is scarcely to be found on this continent. They have a college at * * * that spoils many a man—most of their youth are turned out in a hurry, with a smattering of pretty stuff; and without a solid foundation, pertly set themselves up as the standards of wit, and what is most impudent, of superior judgment. For some time past, I have intended to send, or carry home,* two of my sons for education, and to have consulted you on the subject. My notion is to give them all the useful learning they can take without 'beating it

---

* "Home," formerly a familiar or cant term for England.

into them'—more I do not desire they should have. The languages in the first place, and the mathematics as far as may be. I make it a point they shall learn a method of book-keeping, it is essential to the properly keeping our affairs together, and to check the sallies of extravagant or immethodical men. At this distance, I have no opinion of the great schools in or near great cities. I should be glad the little fellows were led up in a plain manly way, to be fully possessed of useful learning, and not overlooking morals and manners, whatever will tend to make them good men, rather than either worldly saints, or coxcombs, or pedants. Please employ your thoughts for me," &c., &c.

In consequence of Mr. Jenings's subsequent statements and encouragement, the "little fellows" were sent to England the following year, 1767, intrusted to the care of their uncle.

Thomas, aged twelve; Matthias, ten. Their situation there was affectionately attended to by him, who placed them first with a respectable clergyman in the country, afterwards at different preparatory schools, and they finished at Eton College.

In 1771, Mr. Bordley had the affliction to hear of the death of the eldest, Thomas, a remarkably fine and promising youth. He died of consumption. So much was the tender parent attached to this amiable and affectionate child, that he could seldom, even in his latter years, speak of him without tears.

In 1773, he sent over his youngest son, John, then aged nine, under the care of his excellent friend Col. Sharpe. In his pocket-register of that year, is the following memorandum:

"July 10, *Saturday.*

"Son John sailed for England in the Richmond, Captain Love, from the mouth of South River; wind W., and continued fair all Sunday and part of Monday, so that I expect she put out of the Capes Sunday night. Col. Sharpe, Mrs. Ogle, and Sammy Ridout, fellow passengers."

In a letter to his son Matthias, in England, recommending this younger brother to his care, he says: "* * * for what can afford more solid satisfaction than promoting the real interests of our dear connections, at the same time that by it we observe our duty to God!"

In 1766, we find him interesting himself for "young Peale," whom his friendship had followed through various vicissitudes. He now succeeded in gaining a handsome subscription for him, to which he largely contributed, to enable him to visit Europe, to take lessons in painting from his countryman Mr. West, now Sir Benjamin West. Mr. Peale showed his sense of this friendship by attentions to the sons of Mr. Bordley, then in England, and by many subsequent proofs, to himself and family, of his grateful feelings throughout life.

In 1768, Judge Bordley was appointed one of the Commissioners to run the Tangent Line between Maryland and Delaware; and in August of that year, met the other Commissioners at Chestertown, Kent County. Extracts from his own note-book will, perhaps, give the circumstance more clearly, viz.:

"JOURNAL.

"*Sept., Assizes,* 1768, *Eastern Shore.*

"Aug. 24, left home . . . . to meet the Commissioners on the Province Lines, at Chester, Kent County.

"Aug. 28, at Chester.

"Aug. 30, crossed to Col. Lloyd's.

"Aug. 31, left Cambridge. Ben Venables is 16 miles from Vienna, at head of Barren Creek, falling into Nanti-coke, just below Vienna, S° side; near Venables is a swamp; saw the raising of Bogg Iron ore . . . . two miles from Ben Venables is the middle point Stone, or place of begin-ning, to run the Tangent Line towards New Castle, put down by me as a Commissioner directed by the Board."

Mr. Bordley was one of the Governor's Council* during the greater part of the administration of Governor Sharpe, and during the whole of Governor Eden's. There was great intimacy and friendship between him and each of these gentlemen; but particularly with Gov-ernor Horatio Sharpe, whom he never spoke of, even late in life, without terms of strong affection. Perhaps we may trace a portion of this feeling to congeniality of mind and taste in rural concerns. Their intimacy was continued by letter after Mr. Sharpe's return to England, and agri-culture seems to have been the leading theme between them. About a year after the peace between our two countries, Mr. Bordley received a friendly letter from Mr. Sharpe, with the present of a very complete threshing ma-

---

* In Aitkin's Register for 1773, is the following:

"List of the Members of the Proprietor's Council.

The Honorable			Esquires
	Richard Lee,	George Steuart,	
	Benedict Calvert,	William Hayward,	
	Daniel Dulany,	Col. Fitzhugh,	
	John Ridout,	Dan. of St. Thomas Jenifer,	
	John B. Bordley,	George Plater,	

Judge of the Admiralty,

John Beale Bordley, Esq."

The same list is in the Register for 1774—both these are in our possession.

chine, newly invented.   On experiment, he approved of it
highly for a small farm, but found it of no advantage in
threshing his large crops of wheat.

Mr. Bordley's intimacy with Governor Eden was also
uninterrupted and very pleasing, as long as that gentleman
remained in this country; as appears by several friendly
visits made him at Wye, in the course of 1771–2, &c., and
alluded to in the pleasant, easy style of their occasional
correspondence.

An event now occurred which changed the entire future
of Mr. Bordley's views.   His years, and the natural bias
of his disposition, had gradually led him to desire a more
settled life; an inclination still increasing as he gained
further insight into the ways of political men; and perhaps it had reached its greatest earnestness, at the moment
when a delightful retreat was suddenly placed before him!
"Nature, in her cultivated trim," invited him to take possession of a lovely estate on the Eastern Shore of Maryland,
bequeathed to him by his wife's brother, Mr. Philemon
Lloyd Chew.*   It can hardly be supposed that he resisted
the temptation to retire from a political life, offering, at
that period, so little hope to the lover of his country.

We must, however, explain that the circumstances alluded to, which most operated to repel Mr. Bordley from
his honorable and pleasant station on the Western Shore,
were the discovery of various political manœuvres of the
times, and the growing encroachments of the British Gov-

* This gentleman dying a bachelor, left that part of his estate, the beautiful
island at the mouth of Wye River, on which he had resided, to be equally divided between his two sisters, Mrs. Bordley and Mrs. Paca; and to their heirs
it still belongs, 1826.

ernment. These produced disgust, and increasing dissatis-
faction in his warm and upright mind, firm as it always
was, in the best principles of independence. He saw no
opening to better things; no hope then gleamed on the
political horizon, and he decidedly, though not hastily,
drew the conclusion that public life, as then presented to
him, was neither the "Vineyard" where his labors would
be most useful, nor the field where his happiness would
prosper.

Some extracts from his letters may give the clearest
idea of his state of mind, and also of his early and un-
changed political opinions; but in order to understand
some of them, it may be needful to premise, that according
to the circumstances of those times, he was, while holding
the above-mentioned public offices, a great tobacco planter.
This article, then the grand staple of commerce, and
medium of exchange, was cultivated on all the great
Western Shore estates, by means of superintendents or overseers; occasional attention to whom, and to mercantile
accounts and correspondences abroad, interfered but little
with higher concerns. The culture of this plant was then,
and there, the very basis of the means of living; and this
consideration enables us plainly to perceive how sensitive
to their country's honor those men were, who would willingly resign to it, even the resource by which they lived.

To his merchants in London, 1765, there is this expression:

"We must, in case that arbitrary act should be pursued, withdraw our dealings from the other side the water.
What are you now to America? Better withdraw ourselves at once from a ruinous intercourse," &c.

To his brother in London, 1765:

"The warmth of my constitution, when writing last to you on this detestable subject,* hurried me into a violent fret and excessive prolixity," &c.

To his merchants again:

"The late unrighteous attempt upon our property, in the true spirit of Asiatic despotism, entirely changed my scheme of employment, and amongst other acts, I then quitted the public office† which had yielded the most tobacco, and dropped the making of it," &c.

So far back as 1764, he wrote thus to his intimate friend in England:

"We are sensible your Legislature has been too busy with the Colonies, and hope ere this they repent. Were not your late ministers more weighty than wise, and more nice than honest? In matters of such momentous concern as the social happiness of millions, ought we to be diverted from the point, the maintenance of Rights, by notions of delicacy, politeness or fashion?‡

"* * * We, however, less spoilt by foreign and affected education, luxury and venality, see, and with concern, the ruin into which you are running. We expect as a natural consequence of oppression, (whether it begins in Europe or America, it will soon be universal,) that the most virtuous of you will retreat to this as yet uncorrupted, and once (as we hope it will again be) happy country.

"Shall we not also have your best tradesmen and manufacturers? The more you oppress us, the more we must retreat, and learn to live within ourselves. When we no

---

* The Stamp Act.   † The Prothonotary's.

‡ This refers to the refusal of our petitions to the British Parliament, because of some informality in the mode of address.

longer buy your goods, your workmen must want employment, and must go abroad for it. So much has been, and will be said of America, that they will learn they may live here tolerably well on a small farm; but we shall also find looms for them, &c. Well, but you are to send scarlet myrmidons to awe us. Do it; depend on it they will, in no long time, sympathize with us, and become part of us," &c.

Again, to the same:

" We expect to fall off more and more from using your goods; we are already actually the best people; using our old clothes and preparing new of our own manufacture; they will be coarse, but if we add just resentment to necessity, may not a sheepskin make a luxurious jubilee coat?

"Necessity drives us to it; would you have us put up with unprovoked cruelties, and gross insults, and tamely receive a badge of abject slavery without opposition?"

In 1771, he thus writes to the same friend:

"Foppery, idleness, and dissipation are striding briskly on to bring about a general change of proprietors for our lands; the increased cargoes of trash this year imported is astonishing. We must all, from being plain planters and really independent men, turn our eyes to the Court, and gape and beg for places!

"The 'Letters to a friend' is a performance of mine, which I own, rather from the real service it did in my county, (Balt^{re}) at a critical time, when all being in confusion from the effect of the abominable Stamp Act, the magistrates were about to quit their power, than from any other motive."

To his son at Eton College, 1772:

"I wish you may not be put off from your affection for

8

your own country, by growing prejudices, &c. You went away young; don't forget you are a Buckskin; I hope you are an improved one; which is better than to be a spoilt Englishman."

To his friend in London, again:

"Many people here are fortifying their minds for bearing and suffering like men; though others are improvident, and lounge on hope, that all will be well; I wish it, but where is Hope? A tory K——, with all the tory English, and all the other tory nations; all the papists, and in short, all the illiberal, the abandoned and desperate, at his side—against a handful of temperate, liberal, free spirits!"

Many are the similar sentiments pervading his letters, but they are mostly in letters of business, of a nature distinct from politics; in which the prevailing tone of his mind breaks forth in short sentences, or single epithets, which, though most strongly illustrative, because not designed for comment, nor written with a political view, are nevertheless unfavorable for quotation. Enough has been here selected, however, to show the state of disquietude his mind was experiencing for a course of years, and at last some anxious differences arose in the General Assembly, where many of his best friends were concerned, which appear to have wound him up, and fixed him in a resolve to fly from politics forever!

About this time it was, that the beautiful estate at Wye came into his possession, offering him a joyous and irresistible asylum from these public cares. There he removed with his family in 1770; not resigning his offices, nor his influence where it was useful; and continuing his residence for some portion of the year at Annapolis; flattering himself with gradually obtaining a respite from political vexations, which had so strongly impressed his mind, that it could not then cherish any political hopes for his country.

The moment of quitting the Western for the Eastern Shore, was an important era in Mr. Bordley's life. In that remove he exchanged forever a public for a private career, it was his choice to do so; and not more from peculiar inclination than from patriotic feeling. He voluntarily withdrew from the distinctions and the popularity which had thronged upon him in his official course, because, as he himself expressed it, he felt himself in a state of "slavery" to the "British Ministry." Had he remained on the political field of action, until Heaven blessed us with different rulers, we may safely pronounce that he would have been raised to still higher honors, in contributing to exalt the fate of his beloved country; for never had she a citizen with heart more feelingly alive to her rights; more fervently devoted to her interests; he was universally known and acknowledged to be a warm patriot. After his determination to withdraw from public concerns, he was twice called by the general voice of Maryland,* to return to her metropolis and mingle in the management of her public

---

* Once to join the Committee of Public Safety, formed by the Provincial Convention assembled at Annapolis in 1774; afterwards, 1777, when appointed one of the Judges of the *General Court* of Maryland.

In a "History of Maryland" published in 1821, by Thomas W. Griffith; page 65 is the following:

"The members of Council, and of the Upper House, in 1774, and the last under the Proprietary, were Benedict Calvert, John Ridout, John Beale Bordley, George Steuart, Daniel of St. Thomas Jenifer, Benjamin Ogle, Philip Thos. Lee, Daniel Dulaney, William Hayward, William Fitzhugh, George Plater, and Edward Lee, Esquires."

"* * * Mr. Hayward was Chief Justice, and Messrs. Bordley, Jenifer,

affairs; but he considered the objects proposed as merely local and of transient effect, and although aiding them at the time, his general resolution was not to be shaken. At that period, though the spirit of the Revolution was kindled never to be extinguished, action, with any definite or durable plan, was as yet scarcely thought on. Men could not then foresee the rapidly woven tissue of events which afterwards wound around them like an enchanted mantle, and set them at once in the very front and onset of a warfare, so tremendous, and in its end so blessed!

Mr. Bordley's occasional residences in Annapolis still led to constant intercourse with that old home; and his intimate friends, the Carrolls, the Dulanys, the Johnsons, the Jenings, the Scotts, the Brices, &c., &c., &c., still urged every friendly effort to draw him back; he continued to act with them in the Governor's Council, and still retained his judicial station in the Provincial and Admiralty Courts, and joined afterwards in occasional committees when called on; but his mind was made up, his plans were fixed, and

Philip T. Lee, John Leeds, John Cooke, and Jos. Sim, Associate Judges of the Provincial Court."

Page 66.—" As occasion required, Provincial Conventions assembled at Annapolis. The above named gentlemen, with Messrs. Bordley, Jenifer, Thos. Stone, H. Hooper, Charles Carroll, of Carrollton, Edward Lloyd, James Holliday, Thomas Smith, Charles Carroll, Barrister, Richard Lloyd, and Robert Alexander, were appointed a Committee of Correspondence; and they, or some of them, with other eight or nine persons, a Council of Safety, from time to time, until the government under which we now live was organized."

Page 69.—" In the same year, (1777,) &c., Charles Carroll, Barrister, Solomon Wright, and John Beale Bordley, Esquires, were appointed Judges of the General Court; and Thomas ———, Esq., Attorney General."

We have to regret that the author of the above work did not make more complete and copious use of the information, probably before him, in forming his history. He modestly calls it a "Sketch," and so it is; but a full history of Maryland, in those times, is still wanted.

however grateful for these proofs of affectionate esteem in his cotemporaries; and that he was gratefully sensible to them, the writer well remembers to have heard him long afterwards testify; yet, he gradually withdrew himself from the scene of former duty, to one more encouraging to his sense of things; giving some portion of his time to the seat of Government, but more and more to Wye Island.

There he hoped to establish, what he best liked, a life of independence. There, in elegant retirement, adopted into a well educated and affluent circle of neighbors, who commanded from their own estates, with ease, all the comforts and the luxuries of life, he became still more than ever attached to rural life and its concerns, he seemed to find there, his native element; and ere long resigned himself entirely to the plans he had formed, for making himself an Independent American Farmer.

Connected, both by birth and marriage, with many of the first families of the Eastern as well as of the Western Shore, and owning large estates in several different counties of each, he seemed like a connecting link between them; was welcomed and claimed by each; and in fine, always contributed by his respected character, and also by his love of the social tie, to soften and allay the petty jealousies, which sometimes, alas! are wont to arise from local partialities growing into prejudices.

But this delightful harbor from the storms of politics—these pleasant avocations—and these social attractions of good neighborhood, could not make an idle or a selfish being of John Beale Bordley; could not destroy the public-spirited impulses of his heart, nor his strong and firmly cherished sense of duty; never could it be said of him that

8*

he sought for indolent ease! Master of his own actions,
master of a handsome property, it was his choice and the
first wish of his heart, so to employ it as to make it productive of good, not only to individuals, but also to the
community around him ; keeping honor to himself out of
the question, with that genuine modesty for which he was
remarkable, and for which, in those days, there were some
"just spirits" who gave him credit.

Soon after establishing himself at Wye, he proved his
continued interest in the welfare of his country, by endeavoring to promote the spirit of improvement as connected with independence ; and to open the minds of men
of wealth to the advantages, both general and particular,
of enlarged and liberal views. No longer harassed by
conflicting duties, his mind took its own free course in a
cause alike desirable to all; and indulged its warm patriotic feelings, without danger of having its best and fairest
opinions misconstrued by petty interests, or angry collis-
ions. Being a ready penman, he issued from time to time
various useful pieces on public affairs, in the periodical
publications of the day and in handbills ; others that took
the more serious form of essays and pamphlets.

Of these patriotic effusions, few if any are now known ;
their subjects were local and of passing importance, but
their principles and influence were sure and durable.
They were not intended to give celebrity, or any other
personal advantage to their author, they were dictated by
pure feelings, and founded on those palpably just principles which all acknowledge right when placed before them,
though all may not previously see the necessity for setting
them forth to view. These little timely and salutary hints

were known and appreciated at the moment, as being the sentiments of " the Hon. Judge Bordley," whose judicious and impartial habits were well known on both shores of the Chesapeake.

But this honorable title, however well " supported and supporting," he was now voluntarily about to drop, and to assume in its place, that of farmer Bordley, one that, according to his principles, was equally honorable if equally sustained:

" Act well your part, there all the honor lies."

From the moment of taking possession of the Wye Island estate, a farm finely situated, of sixteen hundred acres of good arable land, with a fair proportion of woodland, he turned his attention to husbandry *con amore*. He found a wild, vague and slovenly state of general farming around him; his first step therefore was to educate and qualify himself by studying its elementary principle, and by endeavoring to obtain information from every source worthy of attention.* He sent to England for the best treatises on agriculture, and in the mean time studied, as seriously as ever he had applied to the law, those books on husbandry which he already possessed; for some on this subject, had always found place in his library.† In one of his own latter publications, he says:

* In the course of his researches in the neighborhood, he became acquainted with Mr. John Singleton, an Englishman, comfortably settled on his farm near Easton. Struck with the order and superior cultivation of this estate, Mr. B. commenced an acquaintance and correspondence with Mr. Single ton, and often gladly acknowledged that he had profited much by his practical knowledge, and found Mr. S. a sincere, "intelligent and excellent man."

† In an order to his London merchant for Law books, in 1766, are included the following: " Dr. Elliot's Essays on Field Husbandry;" " Mill's Husby. complete with plates;" "Garret's Designs." And in 1772, again: " Young's 6 weeks tour—I have his other works."

" Mr. Tull's book first excited my attention to agriculture, but to Mr. Young I am obliged for most that I know
of its principles, and of the practices of Europe."

His own extensive practice (on several other farms besides that at Wye) soon enabled him to ascertain how far
they were judicious, and how far suited to the circumstances and climate in which he was acting; thus by an
unwearied and systematic course of observation and reflection, he soon formed theories for himself.

His constant habit, probably acquired when a lawyer,
of taking notes of all he either saw, heard, read, or thought,
that merited attention, was highly serviceable in this pursuit. Tables of directions for times and seasons, and lists
of various work to be executed and given to his overseers
on the different farms, and delivered in at stated periods,
yielded all the usual advantages of order and method, enabled him to trace errors, and diminish the anxiety and
fatigue attending such distant estates,* while they left
more time for particular experiments and improvements
at home.

As he became enlightened himself, he wished to diffuse
the benefits acquired amongst his neighbors; and in endeavoring to wean them from old pernicious habits, he
showed a generous interest, and an earnest desire to promote the spirit of improvement amongst them, which is
still remembered, we are told, by the present descendants
of those old families; and his farming precepts are now
better observed, perhaps, than by those who first received
them. His advances towards others were not likely to be

* The Fancy, Farley, and other Kent County farms—two farms in Harford,
others in Cecil—Pool's Island—Barney's Inheritance—Clagget's Forest, &c.

long resisted, even by the most self-conceited; for there was a nobleness of motive directing them, a patient, untiring system of benevolence, which soon made itself understood—and whether it met with grateful spirits, or unwise spirits, itself was still the same!

Upon some occasion, when one of those busy people, who are always at hand, came to inform him that his neighbor, Mr. ——, had sent his overseer secretly to the Island farm, to pry into his improvements, he answered, "I am heartily glad Mr. —— wishes to improve—my overseer shall invite his to come and look more fully." On some other similar occurrence, when a neighbor expressed regret at some design being copied from him before he had reaped the benefit of it, his reply was, "There is room enough in the world for him and me—and many more such!" At another time he merely answered, "With all my heart!" and then added emphatically Milton's line,

> "Good, the more communicated
> More abundant grows!"

His conduct was consistent with these maxims. One of his practical precepts was to "secure the best seeds;" and to enforce the importance of this on the minds of others, his heart and hand were ever open to supply his neighbors who might be deficient—accompanying each package with a label of directions, or useful hints on culture—generally adding, "remember to preserve the best seed for next year." Every one in his household knew well and contributed to the observance of this rule; the best plants of the different species of fruits and vegetables were carefully ripened for seed, and none but the best. He even once tried the experiment with a small plot of wheat—it was merely for amusement—but fully proved his rule, by the superiority of the next year's produce. On the same principle of always aiming at the best, and of preserving each species distinct, he planted superabundantly of fruit trees, and cut down such as proved inferior—his remarkably fine fruit fully rewarded his care in this instance, as in other particulars of their treatment.

In his subsequent "Notes on Gardening," appended to his "Epitome of Forsyth on Fruit Trees," published in 1803, he says: "In saving seeds, lay out for ten times as much as will be thought wanted; whatever may be above the wants of the garden, it will be a pleasure to supply neighbors with. Till the Editor pursued this principle of economy respecting seeds and fruits he seldom had enough." Again: "The Editor little regarded the breaking down his Peach trees, &c., or their destruction by worms, &c., for he aimed not at 'enough,' but very many times more than enough—in every autumn he planted Peach trees— as regularly as peas are sown in spring!" Again: "Is it not worth the expense to secure such perfect fruit, if it were only for the sick? 'How excellent,' says the good and knowing Tissot,* 'is sound ripe fruit to the sick;' as indeed those who have had it in sickness cannot but remember and vouch!"

His farm soon became conspicuous for its order and general state of perfection: his fences, ditches, gates, roads, and fields, all excited admiration for their substantial excellence, as well as for the neatness which, without any exclusive attention to it, grew out of general method and arrangement. The success of his cultivation was striking;

* Dr. Tissot on Health.

his grain fields were beautiful, and would have been so considered anywhere, but especially in a section of the country whose husbandry from various causes had been much neglected.

On Mr. B.'s first moving to Wye, in 1770, he had begun with attempting the culture of tobacco, still the great staple of commerce. But he found it could not be rendered equal to the Western Shore tobacco; and disliking the crop in every point of view, he soon after discarded it, and resolved to aim at giving supremacy to WHEAT—in which he was ere long completely successful! The soil was favorable; his system of rotations improved this advantage; and in a few years afterwards the Wye River wheat was sought after with avidity by distant merchants. The writer has seen Philadelphia merchant ships, year after year, loading with wheat at Mr. Bordley's wharf—affording him the highest market price. This of course excited emulation— the Maryland white wheat has been long celebrated.*

Mr. Bordley's wheat fields soon attracted general attention; and one season a particular field, of about 300 acres, was so remarkably fine, that its fame spread, and many neighbors crossed the river to view it—amongst them the wealthy and amiable Col. Lloyd, who said jocosely, "Why! Mr. Bordley, your wheat field gains more admiration than my greenhouse!" Coming just then in sight of it, he exclaimed: "and well it may! it is, really, the nobler

* Of the extent of Mr. Bordley's wheat crops we may form some idea at this day, by bills of lading, letters to his merchants, &c. Also, by letters to his brother, Mr. Edmund Jenings, to whom, after his sons were in England, he annually consigned or transmitted the proceeds of some portion of those cargoes for their expenses—the amount of these remittances is seldom under £750 sterling. One shipment of 3000 bushels of wheat to Barcelona brought a net result of £900 sterling.

object to look on!" "And to think on, too!" said Adam Gray, a plain spoken, sensible Scotchman, of their mutual acquaintance as a neighbor.

On changing his general plan of life, Mr. Bordley had entered on, as part of his system, a course of domestic manufactures, embracing multifarious operations, all connected with, though subordinate to, the leading interests of his farm. In this conduct we trace his characteristic independence;—heightened by the desire, early expressed and strongly engrafted on his patriotic feelings, that he might render himself independent of importations from England, in the most essential articles. This plan did not result from private and individual pique or resentment—his feelings led him to act on more generous principles—and in this he was impelled by the hope of doing some good to the community—he trusted that the sentiments and example of one, to whom fortune had given ample means for selecting his mode of life, might have some weight with others; or leave some traces behind, as hints for future improvement by others—and in this modest, unostentatious hope, Time has proved he was judicious.

In tracing the motives of a conduct that differs from the common way of the world, it may be right and just to examine the circumstances by which we estimate it. Let us apply this rule to the case before us. Mr. Bordley was possessed of a very handsome fortune; was of high standing in society, respected for knowledge, sound judgment, and moral life. His feelings and views on the suffering state of his country were warmly patriotic, without the sanguine ardor of youth—they led him to deep and serious reflections on the question then universally felt—what

is to be done? and the answer given by his conduct, as
well as language, was, "Establish independence on the
basis of general industry and invention—we see England
made great by this means—and every excellence attain-
able by human nature must have this foundation." To
give life and evidence to this great truth, we find him at
once resigning many of the luxuries he was habitually fond
of, and voluntarily submitting to privations such as would
raise the tone of complaint from many a spoiled child of
fortune. The annual supplies of luxuries and refinements
which he had always imported from abroad for his family,
now gradually gave place to substitutions which could not
be traced to any common source of gratification; as for one
instance; his taste had been long formed to the relish of the
best London ale and porter, (and in these 'things he was
considered an epicure!) he could not therefore prefer his
own home-made beer.* In proportion as he admired and
valued the imported article, was his desire to see it manu-
factured in our own land. In this there was nothing of a
view to popularity, or the hope of office—he had long enjoyed both, and had retreated from them—besides in those
times there was nothing of a public nature to be obtained,
not even applause, for a conduct that could not then
be understood! His motive, now, is evident; it was a
voluntary sacrifice to the general good. This will appear
more evident from considering the tenor of his life, even
in this incomplete sketch; and those now living who knew
him intimately, will bear testimony in their hearts and

---

* In the article of wine, his plan could not take effect; he was discouraged in
his hopes of success with the *vine* in this country, (though always aiming at it,)
and still imported the best Madeira.

9

memories to the validity of the statement. It was one of
his favorite aphorisms, that "The opinions and voice of
each member of a community, however humble and small,
must tend toward establishing the dominion of either good
or evil." In this view, we may with pride and pleasure
say that his mind still lives in its good effects. Time, and
other causes, have already demolished the solid structures
which, half a century since, he erected with such independent views, but the spirit that suggested them is gone forth—
it was in harmony with that which proclaimed America
free—and was conducive to her best interests through the
gradual but powerful medium of opinion and example.

But we are rambling from our plain narrative. His
little domain soon became an active scene of business and
industry; the numerous buildings rising far and near
around the old-fashioned mansion (whose front extended
one hundred feet) had altogether the appearance of a village; indeed, was generally so considered by passing strangers. There were the carpenter's and blacksmith's shops,
always busy. Looms and spinning-wheels in appropriate
buildings: these prepared all the coarse materials for
laborer's clothing, and were supplied by fleeces from Mr.
Bordley's own flocks, and his own hemp, flax, and cotton.
On another side, a ropewalk, a brickyard and kiln, constructed in 1773; a windmill, built in 1773-4, of uncom-
monly large dimensions and excellent proportions, substan-
tially raised on a stone foundation, surmounted by an
octagon basement on eight brick columns, with an octagon
superstructure of the best timber, tapering towards its
lofty summit, and there finished by a suitable cupola or
head, from one side of which four gigantic arms spread

themselves, revolving, to catch the winds.* On another side, a large brew-house, built of his own bricks, and with great attention to suit the purpose; a double milk-house, also of his home-made bricks, and on a new construction, one story being above ground, the other below, with two rooms in each; on each side spacious areas, over which the roof extended, supported on each side by brick columns eight feet high; a complete two-story brick warehouse, for storing wheat and other grain ready for shipping; a shepherd's house, for an old English herdsman, who received an annuity, and made that his home as long as he lived; a spacious ice-house, smoke-house, store-house, hen-house, pigeon-house, stables, &c., &c., &c.

All these Mr. Bordley constructed in a shorter course of time than might seem probable to many. They involved considerable expense, for they were all on a large scale and designed for durable use—they formed part of a favorite system, he therefore thought little of their cost; and, indeed, in many of them was amply rewarded by their success. The brewery was his greatest hobby, and yielded him most complete satisfaction.† His object in this branch was truly philanthropic—he hoped that, if successful in his own case, it might prove the means of abolishing the general practice, which he considered deplorably pernicious, of giving laborers rum or whisky! It was successful—completely successful—both hired white men and negroes were delighted with the beer he gave them, and became healthier and stronger for the change. His neighbors saw and ad-

* This windmill was a fine object from the mouth of the river, and appears so in a view of the Island, taken in that position by Matthias Bordley, Esq., in 1781.

† We speak of it in connection with his theory of manufactures. Mr. Bordley never sold his beer, or rendered any of his manufactures profitable to himself.

mitted the advantage—and had some professional brewers at that time stepped into the neighborhood, the blessing to the community might have grown and extended. Alas! the chance for it seems now lost!

Previously to trying this favorite project, he applied himself, with his usual assiduous zeal, to study the art of brewing! He appears to have taken up the thought about the year 1778, and in 1781 we find by his books that he had just entered on this new experiment, and that "six Barrells" of "good, stout Beer," were the first result. We have one of his manuscript books, containing a regular statement of his experiments and observations, together with copious extracts from the best publications on the subject, and notes of his conversations with brewers in Philadelphia. It is an interesting document, as showing with what earnestness and good effect he could, even at that period of life, apply his mind to subjects so new to it, and so diversified! It is but justice to the late Judge Bordley to say that the product of his brewery was pure, strong, and wholesome. The writer remembers that in subsequent times, the portion of it set apart for his own table and friends was highly approved of. He continued the practice of giving beer to his people as long as he remained on his farm, and found no cause to regret this judicious project.*

Mr. Bordley very early also turned his attention to manufacturing salt on his own estate, and for this, he looked to the river surrounding it, as in that part it strongly partook of the sea by its junction with the tide-

---

* It ought to have been mentioned that his carpenter was taught to become a good cooper also, and that all Mr. Bordley's barrels were also *home made*.

waters of the bay. By small experiments, he ascertained the quality and quantity to be obtained, and found it sufficiently encouraging with a view to " home consumption," to induce an immediate preparation for that object, thus throwing aside the nice rock and basket salt hitherto annually imported from England. Accordingly, a salt ground was made and all other requisites procured, and his experiments, as we see by his notes and memoranda, proved quite satisfactory, and yielded abundant good wholesome salt. Here again, however, the confusions of the times interrupted his arrangements, and ere they could be re-established, the settled blessings of a free government, happily removed the motive for many of those strenuous efforts, which had their origin in his patriotic wish to be " independent of the dotard mother and her ministers."*

We have also a mill-book journal kept in the same way, with columns for remarks, hints, &c. It serves now to show that same ability for mastering the subject in hand, be it what it might, and also that propensity to mathematical computation which attended all his investigations.

One of the first sentences in his observations on the windmill operations, is a comment on the unusual long " calm" which occurred that season, (1775,) and which " kept work waiting." The mill obtains great praise for its steady behavior in the various purposes for which it was calculated, but whether its expected usefulness diminished, or whether disappointments arose from its being under the direction of a salaried miller, does not appear; but we find that it soon engaged less of Mr. Bordley's attention than other objects. The miller was allowed to

* His own words.

9*

bring in his own books at stated periods; and the original journal which we have referred to, was soon afterwards covered with other memoranda, and with what Mr. B. called his "scribblings," such as comparative estimates, squaring the circle, Archimedes, algebraic problems, rates of exchange, coins, weights, measures, &c., &c. These formed his customary habit for amusement, when with pen, ink, and paper always at hand, he found an interval of leisure, his was a mind that could never be idle.

There is another book in our possession called a "diary," in which he noted all kinds of business connected with the farm; one of the columns headed "employment," another "memorandums," &c. This he began the first year after settling at Wye Island, and continued except when interrupted by the unsettled state of all things and by some long absences from home.

In 1771, Mr. Bordley purchased Pool's Island, in the Chesapeake Bay, about half way between the Susquehanna and the Patapsco, and near to Joppa, his former residence. It contained 234 acres, and it was at the time of purchase, a favorite scheme of his, to bring this spot into a state of improved cultivation according to his best agricultural systems. We have a MS. book of his plans and designs to this effect. He established a good tenant there, who complied tolerably well with some of his directions, and from a perfectly barren wilderness, the land was brought into pretty good cultivation. A good tenant's house erected and a noble barn raised for sheltering a large stock of cattle. This island, at that time, abounded with deer and with remarkably fine wild turkeys. Mr. Bordley endeavored to preserve the race of these animals, and we find directions given to his tenant for this object, expressly forbidding any of the oaks being cut down. In one of his letters to a friend in England, he requests some English hares and partridges to be sent out to him, stating that the climate and situation of this island might suit them. Ample were the arrangements made for this favorite spot. In renting the tenant's house, a stipulated reservation of a "room and a mattrass" for the owner's occasional use, seemed to imply that frequent visits were intended. Little was his mind prepared to expect the great and universal accomplishment of his independent wishes, which soon afterwards roll'd war's thunders all over the continent. Peaceful projects were willingly resigned, and it was the fate of Pool's Island from that time to lose the character of a hobby, and to assume that only of a plain farm, tilled in the common way. Some thirty years afterwards, it yielded a price that may be said to have proved a good reward for a good intention; and in this estimation of the original purchase, let it not be omitted, for it was the circumstance most gratifying to Mr Bordley, that the cattle raised on this island contributed essentially towards those large supplies which he had the happiness to present, at different times, to the armies of his beloved country.

Towards the close of the war, his house at Wye was attacked and pillaged by a band of unprincipled stragglers from the army, called "refugees." They entered the river in the night in boats with muffled oars, one division of the party going to Col. Lloyd's, whilst the other assailed the island house. These gained admittance to the number of twelve; they were armed, masked and otherwise disguised,

they went into the chambers, demanded keys and took possession of everything most valuable, as plate, household
linen, watches, stores of unmade clothing, &c., &c., and
after issuing orders to their men to set fire to one end of
the house, they silently retreated as they came. Happily
the intended fire did not take effect; guilt is easily alarmed,
and hearing something said of the county militia, they
scampered off. Disputing afterwards on the division of
their booty, one of them turned "state's evidence," by
which some articles of value were restored to their owners.

To avoid similar intrusions which the exposed situation
subjected him to, Mr. Bordley removed his family to a
retired rented place, called Galloway, near Easton, where
they passed nearly two years, until the sickliness of the
situation made them gladly return to brave all alarms at
the healthful mouth of Wye.

On removing to the Eastern Shore, Mr. Bordley contract-
ed an intimate acquaintance with Mr. John Cadwalader,
(afterwards General Cadwalader,) who resided partly at
Philadelphia and partly at his estate in Kent County,
called Shrewsbury, from whence he often visited his connections and friends at Wye.

The frank and amiable disposition of this gentleman
soon won Mr. Bordley's friendship, and though considerably
younger than Mr. Bordley, their intimacy gained ground
with every succeeding year up to the lamented early death
of Gen. Cadwalader, in 1785. His friend left Wye to attend
him in his last moments, at Shrewsbury, and grieved sincerely over his grave. This intimacy has been thus particularly noticed because of its apparent, though indirect
influence on some parts of Mr. Bordley's future life, as will
appear in subsequent events.

In the spring of 1773, Mr. and Mrs. Bordley placed their daughter Henrietta Maria at the best school in Philadelphia, on the earnest recommendation of Mr. and Mrs. Cadwalader. To Mrs. Cadwalader, the General's first wife, she was distantly related on the mother's side. She was then at the tender age of eleven, and gratefully received the unlimited and unremitted kindness of those esteemed friends, thus riveting the parent's friendship.

It was in the autumn of this year, that Mr. Bordley was deprived of a consort to whom he had been united twenty-two years. After a lingering illness, and on her return homewards from a visit to her daughter and for her health, in Philadelphia, she died at Chestertown, Maryland, on the 11th of November, 1773, and was buried in the Bordley family vault at Annapolis.

Mr. Bordley appears to have been duly sensible to this bereavement. He was not a man of profession or ostentation in anything, but we may gather something of his way of thinking and acting by a letter of his now before us, written some time after the above event, to an elderly lady, a friend of his late wife, an extract from which may better demonstrate his mind than any terms of our own, and it will particularly show how, in him, sentiment was connected with conduct.

" Madam ——, no gratification of the mind within my experience, is equal to what arises from a dutiful and affectionate attention to the memory of a departed friend. Such attention is free from flattery, there being no possibility of any return from the deceased, but it carries its own reward, a secret inexpressible satisfaction. With the survivor, it is well, if accident throws it in his way to ena-

ble him to meet this duty, to do in memory of his departed friend, what it may be supposed, he or she would have
done. It is too seldom such opportunities occur, and sometimes they are unwarily overlooked.

. " For the civilities you were pleased to show my wife,
when she came a stranger to Wye, she was much obliged
to you, and greatly esteemed you, ... she has left me
to make you this acknowledgment, tho' but a poor repre-
sentative of her grateful mind," &c.

After this event, it became still more important to fix
his daughter at school, and he reconducted her to Philadelphia and again commended her to the friendly eye of Mr.
and Mrs. Cadwalader.

During his frequent preceding and subsequent visits to
Philadelphia, Mr. Bordley passed many happy days with his
friends, the Cadwaladers, both in that city and at Shrewsbury, particularly in the hospitable case of Maryland manners at the latter place. And General Cadwalader's regard also led Mr. Bordley to find his house in Philadelphia
like a home; there, besides seeing his little daughter to advantage, he often met the best society of the city, with
some of whom he was previously acquainted, with others
became so, and strengthened the link of fellowship with
such as he preferred. A few of these old names now appear before us in irregular memoranda; we find in one
of his pocket registers for 1773, viz. :

" April 20. To Phila :—Cadwalader's—friendly club
or rout at Mrs. C——'s—Dr. Cadwalader—Mr. Willing
—Morris—Powel—Col. Fell—their ladies—and Mrs. Penn
—Mrs. Masters—Miss Masters—very sociable.

"21. Governor's club—Mr. Hamilton—Mr. Gibson* (Mayor)—Dr. Cadwalader—Mr. Inglis—John & Lambert Cadwalader—Mr. Humphries—R. Tilghman—S. Meredith—&c.

"22. Dr. Cadwalader's—dine—&c.

"24 Merchant's club—Mr. Hill—Mr. Nesbit—Cox, the lawyer—D. Beveridge, &c., &c.

"25. Mr. Hamilton's—dine—Jo. Pemberton—&c."

In this respectable and select society Mr. Bordley passed the principal part of his time, during his frequent visits to Philadelphia on his little daughter's account. In process of time these visits became more frequent, and it is necessary we should explain why they were so. Amongst those valuable acquaintances he often heard mentioned, and sometimes met, the widow Mifflin,† whom he found much beloved and respected, and always spoken of in terms that marked high regard. He heard her praised for her good sense, good temper, candor and prudence, by persons who were cautious how they spoke of others; and they commended her for her judicious care of her son,

---

* John Gibson, Esq., one of the members of the Governor's club, was also for several years Mayor of the city, at that time. After the formation of the new government, he was the first Auditor-General of the United States Treasury, and continued so until he resigned this office, in 1780. He was the father of the present James Gibson, Esq., Counselor-at-Law. 1826. Philadelphia.

† Her maiden name was Sarah Fishbourne. She was daughter of William Fishbourne, Mayor of the city of Philadelphia from 1718 to 1722. Her mother's maiden name was Jane Roberts, who married first William Fishbourne, and afterwards John Galloway, Esq., of West River, Maryland; there her daughter Sarah resided until she attained her thirteenth year, when her mother died—about 1745 or 1746—and she removed to Philadelphia, to *put herself* to the best schools. She also entirely superintended the education of her young sister, Jane Galloway, who afterwards married Joseph Shippen, Esq., of Philadelphia.

John F. Mifflin, born after his father's death, and of her
step-son, Thomas Mifflin, (afterwards Governor of Pennsylvania,) as also for the rational plan, ease and comfort of
her mode of life, and her discreet management of a handsome property. They mentioned a fact which forcibly
proved the unostentatious and solid principles of this lady,
which deserves to be repeated for the credit of her sex.
Her husband left her, by will, his handsome double house,
completely furnished, at the corner of Chestnut and Front
Streets, (then the fashionable quarter of the town,) with
ample means for supporting it; but she thought it too
large and too public for the proposed retirement of her
widowed condition, and sold it; at the same time building
herself an excellent single house on her patrimonial estate
on Union Street. There she resided sixteen years, bending
her whole mind, time, and means to the liberal education
of her son, and only diversifying the subject by true social
intercourse with a few intimate friends, such as deserved
to be so considered, who earnestly sought communion of
mind with her, and willingly aided her meritorious endeavors. Amongst these "chosen few" was Mrs. Chew,
(the first wife of Benjamin Chew, Esq., of Philadelphia;
she was a Miss Galloway, of Maryland;) Mrs. Hester
White, (the mother of the present Bishop White;) Mrs.
Anne Penn, (wife of Governor John Penn;) Miss Allen,
(her sister;) Miss Anne Meredith, (afterwards Mrs. Hill;)
the Cadwaladers, Dickinsons, Clymers, Shippens, &c., and
also most of the excellent amongst the people called
Quakers, with whom she was connected by her mother's
and husband's families. But although she highly respected

and esteemed the Quakers, she never joined their religious society.*

Whilst on the subject of this lady, we feel it due to her in justice to say, that although many of her most intimate friends in that day were of the Tory party, she was herself uniformly and decidedly a Whig. None of that refreshing luxury, *Tea*, was used in her house throughout the national contest ; her patriotic sentiments were never withheld from those friends of the other side; yet they respected her to the last. With Mrs. Anne Penn, who survived most of the others, the intimacy continued through life, and was supported by letters across the Atlantic.

In the course of his Philadelphia visits, Mr. Bordley visited in the family of Col. White, (father of our venerated Bishop White.) They were originally from Maryland, and already well known to him. Here he sometimes met this same widow Mifflin, and he could not fail to observe that she was a distinguished favorite with Mrs. White, whose judgment and goodness he equally respected. With such claims to respectful attention, joined to an engaging address and appearance, Mrs. Mifflin soon be-

---

* Lest some might consider this as indicating a want of religious thought, we will mention two little facts that are to the subject. Whilst she was yet quite a young woman, and her own mistress, a deputation from this respectable society waited on her with spiritual advice, and amongst other things recommended her to wear a plain cap, saying that " it would be more becoming to her." She answered, " For that reason, I ought not to put it on !"

When afterwards a widow, a similar deputation waited on her to speak to her respecting her son, his father having been a member of their society : and they earnestly recommended her to give him a religious education. Her answer to them was, " I agree with you perfectly, my friends, and I take my son constantly to church, and teach him his Bible and his catechism." They generously replied, " We respect thy candor !"

10

came the object of Mr. Bordley's devoted attachment. Her friends were his friends, and anxious for his success. In short, they were married, by the Right Reverend Bishop White, October 8, 1776.

In consenting thus to renounce her settled mode of life, her early friends, and her interesting son, just seventeen, to seek a distant home, new faces, new habits and unknown difficulties, this lady clearly proved her respect for, and her confidence in such merit as she saw in Mr. Bordley. If we were writing her life, we might have much to say, both narrative and descriptive—we might demonstrate her habitual truth, her cultivated affections, her charity in its enlarged Christian sense, including a love of justice, her pious humility, her patient fortitude—but we will refrain, and content ourselves with remarking that she faithfully acquitted herself of her new duties ; that she in time overcame the prejudices of some against her as a stranger, engrafting affection in their place by the beautiful moral consistency of her conduct; and that she proved throughout their union, a blessing to Mr. Bordley and his family.

After his marriage, one of Mr. Bordley's first measures was to give up to his wife's son, John F. Mifflin, then seventeen, all the property that she would, by a marriage settlement, eventually intend for him. It was held in trust until he was of age, when he took possession of it, and was affectionately sensible to the generous feeling that suggested this conduct.

And now came on the "trying times" of the war! Whilst Mr. and Mrs. Bordley were on a visit to his family and friends in Annapolis, a report that the British fleet was rapidly approaching that city, sent the unprepared

inhabitants scampering off in every direction. Mr. Bordley packed off as many as possible in his stout London-
built coach, which flying as fast as such a heavy vehicle
could be said to fly, even with four horses, it was over-
turned in the darkness of night, the ladies narrowly
escaping with their lives. Happily the dawn of day
brought the joyous discovery that the fleet had changed
its destination, and was retreating down the bay, allowing
the beautiful sight of twenty-seven well-rigged men-of-war
in full sail, to be quietly enjoyed. After this, Mr. Bordley
remained some time longer in Annapolis, anxiously assisting
in concerting measures for the general safety.

On the 21st of October, 1777, news of the capture of
Burgoyne reached Annapolis by express; and on that day,
amidst the rejoicing tumult of bells and cannon, Mrs.
Bordley presented her husband with a little daughter,
afterwards baptized by the name of Elizabeth. This was
their only child.

About a year from that time Mr. Bordley restored his
family to his favorite residence at Wye, there to pursue
his former well-arranged plans, and to add to them an
object of new and increasing interest. This was to lay by
a stock of provisions for our nobly struggling army. In
pursuance of this plan, Mr. Bordley every now and then
sent off to some of the military stations the present of a
boat load of beef, flour, vegetables and fruit, the produce
of his own farms. He thus indulged his humane disposition, while at the same time he contributed, largely and
joyfully, throughout the war, to support the general cause.
No charge having ever been made for these supplies, there
is probably no record or public document of them. There

are still a few persons living who remember these circumstances. Amongst them is Mr. Bordley's daughter, Mrs.
Henrietta Maria Ross, who expresses her remembrance of
them thus :

"I perfectly remember my father presenting, for the
use of the army, a number of beeves and a quantity of
wheat. I can't remember exactly the time, but I think it
was about '77 or '78, at a time when the army were
suffering for provisions.   HENRIETTA M. Ross."

In 1783 Mr. Bordley was elected a member of the
"American Philosophical Society." When, in later years,
he removed to Philadelphia, he derived much satisfaction
in attending the meetings of this society, composed as it
was of men of distinction for abilities and knowledge.

Mr. Bordley now resided more permanently at Wye
Island, and steadily continued his agricultural experiments
and improvements. As his systems became matured, he
published their results: at first on written cards, sent
around his neighborhood, then in printed handbills, of
which we have two, one called "Country Economy," another "Farmyard Economy;" and in 1783-4, his small
essay, entitled "Summary View of Courses of Crops, &c.,"
which he presented liberally through the country. His
object in so doing was to rouse those farmers who lived by
the soil to make exertions for themselves ; he therefore endeavored to place before them, in precept as well as practice, the dignity and importance of agriculture, and the
improvements it was susceptible of, when justly considered.
We have seen with what enthusiasm his mind early attached
itself to this object—the country and rural concerns were,

at every period of life, his greatest delight—it seemed as
though they held the master-key to his intellectual existence, and that whatever general or diversified knowledge
he imbibed, became tributary to that leading prepossession.
As he advanced in life, and cast his view around on what
he called "the great landed interest of our nation," he
became more alive to the value of agriculture as an object
of general importance; and connecting the encouragement
of it with the Christian's duty of "doing good," and the
principle that each voice in the community has its influence, he commenced, as we have seen, in his own neighborhood, and by his own individual exertions. But he began
to fear that these efforts failed of producing the durable
impression he desired;—it was a subject on which every
small farmer thought himself already qualified to judge,
or sufficiently informed for his own purposes. The lazy
maxim, " 'twill do well enough," was a bar to improvement
that Mr. Bordley full often complained of—but he found
it unconquerable, for want of a visible excitement—either
to gratify honest pride, or emulative interest.

To lead the way to better results, he now conceived the
idea, during his long winter retirements at Wye, of forming a Society amongst well-informed men of liberal minds,
for promoting agricultural knowledge, and exciting a spirit
of improvement. His own native State, however, did not
at that time favor such an establishment. He communi
cated freely with those most likely to understand the
subject, and found them not to be roused: on the Western
Shore, the universal and settled culture of tobacco im-
peded such an object: on the Eastern Shore, the men of
enlarged views lived then too scattering and too remote

10*

from any eligible center of union, and all others were too supine.

In consequence of these discouraging circumstances immediately around him, he determined on resorting to a city for the benefit of the country, and to set the idea of his project afloat in Philadelphia on his next visit there. He hinted this plan in his correspondence with his step-son, Mr. Mifflin, and endeavored to obtain through him an insight into the characters most likely to favor and support the scheme, viz., "men of property and education, not tied down by professional engagements or local prejudices, and prone to feel an interest, either general or particular, in the suggested institution."

Accordingly, in visiting Philadelphia in the winter of 1784–5, he introduced the idea of his favorite project in a small intimate circle, and had the pleasure to find that it excited an interest; particularly in his friend, Mr. Powel, whose active mind, not shackled by the cares of business nor biased by conflicting interests, at once caught a view of its general advantages, and agreed to support it with his best endeavors.

It was soon afterwards determined to have a meeting of those who favored the proposed scheme, and to ascertain the names of such others as might wish to become joint members. Accordingly, with a book for minutes on their table, they met, with a view to concert more formal measures, on February 11, 1785. The preamble to these, their first minutes, is in Mr. Bordley's handwriting, and runs thus:

"City of Philadelphia, Feb. 11, 1785.

"In conversation on the subject of agriculture, and the promoting improvements therein, within the States of America, it was proposed to form a Society for that purpose, to be held in the city of Philadelphia; and thereupon,

Messrs.

George Morgan,	Benj. Rush (M.D.),
George Clymer,	Samuel Meredith,
Robert Morris,	Jno. Nixon,
Jno. Cadwalader,	Charles Thompson,
Henry Hill,	Richard Wells,
Philn. Dickinson,	Jno. Jones (Phys.),
James Wilson,	Adam Kuhn (Phys.),
Thomas Willing,	Lamt. Cadwalader,
Samuel Powel,	Richard Peters,
Edward Shippen,	Doctor Geo. Logan,
Samuel Vaughan,	and
Tench Francis,	Jno. B. Bordley—(23)

"in number twenty-three, were agreed and nominated to be the members thereof: who, or such of them as should meet for the purpose, should form a set of Laws for regulating the Society, and also elect, according to such Laws, other members, and honorary members. In pursuance whereof,

"At the house of Patrick Byrne, in front street, in the city of Philadelphia on tuesday the first day of March, 1785, were present:

Mr. Clymer,	Mr. Francis,
—— Powel,	—— Rush,
—— Shippen,	—— Logan,
—— Vaughan,	—— Bordley,

"who made choice of Mr. Powel for their Chairman: and after some general consideration of the views of the Society, they appointed Mr. Clymer and Mr. Bordley to sketch out a form of Laws to be presented at the next meeting, at this place, on the next Tuesday."

It was afterwards proposed to appoint Mr. Bordley their President, but having himself been the prime mover of the design of the Society, he, with his accustomed delicacy, declined that honor. Mr. Powel was then nominated and elected President, and Mr. Bordley Vice-President, which stations they both retained till their deaths. The minutes being then and for some time in his own writing, this first nomination for President does not appear on them, but it is a fact well remembered by his family. They also well recollect to have heard him repeatedly called the *Father* of the Agricultural Society of Philadelphia.

The immediate and unexampled success of this Society was calculated to give the purest delight to such a mind as Mr. Bordley's; he had the pleasure to see the first men in the nation* joining their names and their interests, and

---

* Amongst these, in the list of members besides those above mentioned, are

Benjamin Franklin,	William White (Rt. Rev.),
Timothy Pickering,	Arthur St. Clair,
Thomas Bond (M. D.),	Edward Burd,
Samuel Vaughan and sons,	John Penn (senior),
Casper Wistar (M. D.),	John Penn (junior),
Samuel Morris (Christian),	William Hamilton,
S. P. Griffitts (M. D.),	Robert Hare,
Thomas and John F. Mifflin,	Thomas Willing,
Robert Milligan,	William Bingham.

And amongst a long list of Honorary Members, are

General Washington,	Danl. & Chas. Carroll, Maryd.
Bushrod Washington, Vir.	Philp Schuyler, NY.
Oliver Wolcot, Con.	Edmund Jenings, London.

giving their presence to encourage the views of this infant institution, and this with alacrity and earnestness, as men aware of the intrinsic value of the object aimed at; for they saw and felt that it was not instigated by private ambition or selfishness—they saw that public good was its end and aim. Men who had risked their lives and fortunes for that same public good, in war, were equally ready to sustain the noble principle in all its branches under the blessings of peace; and who shall say that the fruits of Agriculture are not first on the list?

Yes! Mr. Bordley rejoiced in the success of his darling project; he ardently hoped that so auspiciously protected, it might long pursue the "even tenor of its way," unbiased by party influence or selfish intrigue; it was his plain honest wish to see it support itself, by its own merits and usefulness: leading the way to the diffusion of knowledge on a subject so closely connected with the general welfare of this great country, that he considered it not only as the "spinal marrow of its existence," but when rightly understood, and pursued by enlightened minds, as the best basis for virtue and happiness on earth.

James Bowdoin, Massts.	Edward Lloyd, Maryd.
George Clinton, NYork.	John Langdon, N. Hamp.
John Jay, Jer., & Philp van-Ran-	Richard Penn, London.
sclaer. NY.	Gouverneur Morris, NY.
Rt. Revd. R. Smith, S. C.	William Paca, Maryd.
Baron Steuben,	Temple Franklin.
Ant. Wayne, Pen.	John Rutledge, S. C.
Jer. Wadsworth, Con.	Edward De Courcey, Maryd.
Dr. John Warren. Mass.	Robt. Browne, Maryd.
Ralph Izard. S. C.	John Singleton, Maryd.
Genl. N. Greene, Rd. Isd.	William Hemsley, Maryd.
Robt. R. Livingston, NY.	Charles Carter, Virga.
Benjn. Lincoln, Mass.	Major David Ross, Maryd.
Genl. Henry Knox,	William Hayward, Maryd.

Having no vain wish to gain applause or distinction, Mr. Bordley no longer interfered with the regulations of the Society; having seen it safely launched, he conceived his principal duty done, and was contented to resign it to its appointed commander and officers; and also, provided it did but exist, content to have it forgotten that he was its founder—or, perhaps, trusting for that remembrance to the justice of his cotemporaries, he was the more regardless of it himself. He received many letters* of congratulation and compliment on the success of his generous labors for the promotion of agriculture; he regarded them no further than as expressive of the writer's good-will, and as sustaining his hope that in time men would universally learn to "venerate the plough."

In the course of years, Mr. Bordley and some other members observed what they considered defects in the construction of the Society; and the lamented death of their first President, Mr. Powel, in 1793, together with his own actual residence in Philadelphia having thrown greater responsibility on him as Vice-President, he suggested various new regulations amongst those of his friends most interested in the subject, and issued repeated notices† calling a meeting of the Society; but the fatal yellow fever of that year had paralyzed exertion, and these calls were for some time in vain, until January 14, 1794, when a circular signed by Mr. Bordley as Vice-President, appointed the 21st January for a special meeting on two important objects, which were

---

* One of these was from Arthur Young, Esq., addressed to Mr. Bordley, as "President of the Society, &c.," and accompanied by the present of a set of his Annals of Agriculture.

† These having been printed, we have still a number of them.

1st. To petition the Legislature for an act of Incorporation.

2d. To prepare outlines of a plan for establishing a State Society for the promotion of agriculture.

Both which were done by the Committee appointed, viz., Messrs. Bordley, Clymer, Peters, and Pickering. The petitions were presented to the Legislature, and "nothing more was done." Mr. Bordley adds a remark, that "the application was rejected by husbandmen, who were principally to be benefited!"

The minutes of these meetings and transactions appear in Mr. Bordley's last work on "Husbandry," published by him in 1799.

From that period, there seems to have been an interruption to the meetings of the society, the cause of which does not appear. Alas! "tares" will forever "grow up with the wheat" of human planting. Mr. Bordley had the mortification to see petty interests and individual vanity tarnishing the fair luster of this well-founded institution. And under these circumstances, the refusal of the Legislature to give it their sanction and aid, was peculiarly wounding to his feelings, and drew forth the above exclamation.*

In pursuing the details connected with the establishment of this interesting society, we have advanced beyond the regular narrative, and must now return to it. Mr. Bordley's mind was not wholly engrossed by agriculture, it was always open to subjects of general interest to the

---

* The remnant of this society was again rallied in 1805, the year following Mr. Bordley's decease, when Mr. Bordley's particular friend, George Clymer, Esq., was elected Vice-President, and Judge Peters, President. (See their minutes in the 1st volume of minutes.)

community. He had long observed and lamented so far back
as when he was Prothonotary in Baltimore County, the unsettled and vague state of our currency his papers, books,
letters, &c. are full of calculations, comparisons, and observations on the different currencies and coins of the commer-
cial world, pointing out the necessity for an improved system
of our own.　With this view, he entered into correspondence with some of the first financial characters of our country, and we believe was one of the first who proposed the
adoption of the decimal division of our moneys.　It is well
known that he was one of its warmest advocates.　In 1789,
he published a small piece on "Moneys, Coins, Weights,
and Measures," and in 1790, a "Supplement" to it; these
were designed to awaken the attention of such as were
ignorant (and in that day they formed the bulk of the people) of the advantages arising from our newly appointed
system.　He also published, in 1790, a small essay on
"National Credit and Character," intended to point out
in an easy and familiar manner, the real interests and great
advantages of our new government.　To appreciate the
object of these little pieces, we must recollect, they were
written when reading was not so general as it has since
become, and when, of course, there existed the danger of
that discontent which is the growth of ignorance, some
symptoms of which he perceived, and therefore distributed
these timely hints.　In 1793, Mr. Bordley wrote and published a small piece on "Yellow Fever."　In 1794, he also
wrote and published "Intimations on Manufactures, Agriculture, and Trade."　In 1797, "Sketches on Rotations of
Crops."　In 1798, "On Pasturing Cattle."　In 1797,
"Queries from the Board of Agriculture of London, with
Answers by J. B. Bordley."　In 1799, "On Hemp," with

a supplement. In 1800, " Husbandry dependent on Live-
stock." In 1799, his largest work on husbandry, called
" Essays and Notes," &c., consisting of six hundred and
forty-six pages ; and in 1803, an " Epitome of Forsyth on
Fruit Trees, with notes by an American Farmer."

We have thus endeavored to collect together some of
the various topics on which he employed his pen, though
well aware, that the catalogue is very incomplete. So little consequence did Mr. Bordley attach to anything but
the object immediately in view by these productions, that
few of them have been preserved, even in his own family.
Of those above named we have copies. That Mr. Bordley's
motive in writing may be justly understood, we must here
mention, that he did not wield the pen of a " fine writer."
It was not for his own amusement that he undertook these
publications ; for he always confessed that he had not done
justice to his own intentions by them, for, as he expressed
it, " I write too much on the spur of the occasion."

It is now time to give a slight view of Mr. Bordley's
domestic life, as passed in later years at Wye Island : we
have no knowledge of it in any preceding period. There,
both he and Mrs. Bordley collected together, every summer, as many of their mutual relations and connections as
possible, inviting them cordially to come and partake with
them of the luxuries which both nature and cultivation
there yielded abundantly in that blest season of fruits and
flowers.* Of the constant and regular members of the

---

* Besides the ample products of Mr. Bordley's farm and garden, the river
yielded in profusion and in perfection, every variety of *fish*, from the rich
sheep's-head and rock-fish, down to the sparkling diamond-fish, and sweet cro-
cus and the fat crab, with and without its shell. In winter, this spot also
yielded every variety of wild-fowl.

summer circle, who were absentees in winter, was Miss
Bordley, Mr. Bordley's sister, who resided in Annapolis,
and his daughter Henrietta Maria, who in 1781 married
Major David Ross,* of the Western Shore of Maryland, and
resided at Bladensburg. Miss Bordley was often accompanied by some of her distant female relations, and Mrs.
Ross, in the course of time, brought a merry little troop of
children to feast on grandpapa's fine fruit.

His son Matthias still made his home with his father,
and it was predicted of him, from his steady habits, that he
would live and die a bachelor.† His son John married
soon after his return from Europe, and settled near Chestertown, Kent County. Mr. Bordley's step-son, John F.
Mifflin, of Philadelphia, occasionally left his city avocations to visit his mother in her rural home. Add to these
accidental visitors, who were liable to come in the genuine old Maryland way from every point of the compass, and
there was assembled always a happy, often a large company, amusing themselves as they liked best in the luxurious ease of Maryland hospitality ; most of them remaining from May to November, any occasional vacancies being
soon filled up.

With his neighbors, Mr. Bordley uniformly preserved
the pleasantest terms of social ease and friendliness. Frequent interchange of civilities with the Pacas, the Lloyds,
the Tilghmans, the Goldsboroughs, the Hollidays, the Hay-
wards, the Chamberlains, the Blakes, the Brownes, the
Hemsleys, the Hindmans, &c., kept up through the fair

* Major Ross attained his military rank by well sustained service in the
Revolutionary War.

† That was not the age of prophecy. Matthias married Miss Susan Heath in
1799, and has now thirteen children.

season, a busy succession of visitings, dinners, and various
convivial meetings. These, with neighborly attentions,
fruit to the sick, &c., kept the batteaux and canoes constantly plying, and banished every unpleasant thought of
being on an island. Visitors to Mr. Bordley not unfre-
quently came from the Western Shore, as for instance, Gov.
Plater and his charming family, the Brices, the Ridouts,
&c. Sometimes they came from other States, as Mr.
Bordley's intimate friend, Bishop Smith, of South Caro-
lina, whose last visit, with his family, was of two weeks,
previous to sailing for Europe. Doctor Geo. Logan, of
Philadelphia, in 1786 or 1787, with his charming and
exemplary wife, made a visit of ten days, and being a lover
of farming, passed the time to his satisfaction in examining Mr. Bordley's improvements, and many others not now
recollected.

Mr. Bordley was an early riser; his duties and plans for
the day were arranged in a system before him. His first
step was to his garden, distant about one hundred yards
from the house. This was a finely varied piece of ground
of eight acres, selected and surveyed by himself. In laying it out, he perhaps attended more to the useful than
the beautiful, and yet three large avenues, diverging from
the main entrance to the extremities, bordered on each
side with the finest fruit trees, bending under the weight
of blushing and golden treasures, and interspersed by flow-
ering shrubs, may be said to possess some beauty. Here
he generally passed an hour and a half, or two hours, in
giving directions to the head gardener, omitting nothing;
and this done, he filled the remaining interval of time with
exercise and thought, giving free range to those pious
meditations which the hour and the scene promoted.

He was fond of pruning and grafting, and in the proper seasons, himself took charge of the choice fruits and vines that required those offices. He cultivated the grape with care, and formed two complete vineyards with soil artificially made for the purpose. He imported the celebrated Tokay grape, in the hope it might suit our climate, and raised it to bear fruit which proved its superior flavor for a wine grape; he, however, experienced some discouragement in the culture of it we believe, from the dryness of our summers. He raised also the nectarine, but not to perfection; but his peaches, melons, pears, and plums were so incomparably fine that he was indifferent to that one inferior variety.

The fig, of various sorts and in luscious abundance, found a genial climate and soil in his garden; the ruddy pomegranate too was there, though slightly prized amidst its more valued neighbors. The sweet almond also, Mr. Bordley raised to advantage, both in Maryland and Pennsylvania, and endeavored to induce others to do so.* His attention was not confined to fruit; whatever, in the course of his diffusive reading, he met with worthy to be introduced into culture for general advantage, he immediately endeavored to procure, and first gave a place in his garden for a fair experiment. In this point of view, he early raised there the palma-christi, and succeeded in expressing good oil from it, recommending it as an article of trade to those who had small farms. He also gave a place in

---

* In his " Notes on Gardening" to the Epitome of Forsyth, p. 146, he thus mentions it: " The Editor chose the coldest, most airy, exposed, and clayey part of his garden, where he planted Almonds. The trees bore fruit to perfection in three years after planting the nuts; they were the large soft shelled Almond."

his garden to the madder plant for several years previous to his leaving Wye—the writer well remembers his calling the attention of his visitors to a large bed of this favorite plant which he had procured through a friend in England, of the best sort, and expressing his great pleasure in seeing it thrive so vigorously in our climate ; one of the gentlemen coldly asked him, "Why he suffered it to occupy so much of his garden and his attention ?" The writer well remembers his emphatic answer, "Sir, this will one day be a manufacturing country, and then, that little plant will be invaluable." Alas ! there were but very few who could thus generously anticipate for the public good.* These morning visits to his garden interested Mr. Bordley so much, that it was often necessary to dispatch a little messenger a second time to say "Breakfast is ready, sir !" And he has been often known to be unconscious of a pattering shower until roused by the arrival of an umbrella, which, however, he generally discarded and sent back with his "compliments to the ladies." In fruit season, his return to the family was attended by large baskets loaded

---

* In the " Notes" to his large work on " Husbandry," he mentions this plant, and adds: " In my garden at Wye, I was much pleased with the growth and produce of a bed of Mr. Arbuthnot's choicest kind of Madder, and wished to spread the culture of it amongst country families who appeared the most concerned in little domestic manufacturing. But, alas ! only one family desired to have of it, and planted some roots in their garden." Mr. Bordley also raised annually in his garden, a considerable number of hop vines of that superior kind called the *Farnham Hop*, to which he was attached for many reasons. He thus mentions it in the work on Husbandry, page 395: "This hop was introduced into Maryland by that patttern of manly virtues, the late Mr. Sharpe, when he was Governor of Maryland. Some of the roots he gave me, and I planted of them 250 hills," &c. Mr. Bordley took great pains to introduce this hop into Pennsylvania, and left them with directions at Como, his farm in Chester County, bought by Dr. McCloud.

11*

with every variety of Pomona's choicest gifts, fully well ripened and nicely culled.*

After breakfast, his horse or his chaise were daily in waiting at the door, and he instantly set out for the more important superintendence of his farm. The farmyard, the principal scene of business, was distant a mile from the mansion house; there he spent some time in consultation with his overseer, explaining and directing according to his various plans and wishes; he then went round to his people's quarters, and listened to their various wants, or gave them useful hints that suited their capacities—then he drove round to his different manufactories, viewed his extensive fields, flocks, &c., and thus occupied the whole forenoon and part of the afternoon. He generally went prepared with medicine or some little comforts for his poor black people, which he made it a point to have ready each night before going to bed. He kept a constant stock of all necessaries for the sick, and in time became such a skillful practitioner as seldom to need a physician—many instances occurred where he recovered them from extreme danger, and they preferred his treatment to any other.

About two o'clock he returned home to prepare for din-

* This fruit was for the day's use, first beginning with the breakfast table, and not forgetting neighbors. The baskets were first placed on the floor of the hall, until disposed of. As in Mr. and Mrs. Bordley's plan of education, obedience and self-denial were taught to " grow with the growth" in " spirit and in truth," thereby precluding the necessity of punishment—we cannot omit mentioning an instance that proves the complete success of their theory : one of their children, then two years old, was told not to touch the above fruit placed on the floor; she was seen soon afterwards, playing and dancing around the baskets, quite alone, with her hands put behind her, as if to keep them from touching it. Would to Heaven our full-grown obedience to our Heavenly Father could be like that of well-trained " little children," how much more happiness might this world exhibit !

ner; exchanging his coat for a dressing-gown, he took a draught, already prepared, of what he called a "cool tankard,"* or a bowl of lemon punch, and when fatigued or heated, threw himself for a few moments on a bed or old-fashioned settee, and then rose to shave, have his hair dressed, &c.†

At his social board, no one could be more truly social; it was amply supplied with well prepared viands, and seasoned by cheerful gratitude to Heaven, and love to our neighbor on earth, while the example of those who presided, set the tone of harmony, ease and enjoyment to all around. The younger branches of the family who were admitted to these meals, saw and learnt to love the simple, happy exercise of the Christian virtues: patience, modesty, respect for the rights of others, sympathy, generosity, self-respect, discretion, temperance, good humor and gratitude, all successively came into action, and on proper occasions were pointed out, explained, and commended; and became engrafted on the subject with the ease of habit—that second nature, which gives to civilization its best graces.‡

The cloth removed, the children's whispered grace, "Thank God!" responded, and they sent merrily off with

* "A cool tankard" was simply wine sangaree with sprigs of balm and burnet in it, cooled with ice.

† In those days gentlemen tied their hair in a queue, and dressed it with powder and pomatum.

‡ Perhaps it may be observed that all this might be summed up in the word politeness, yet politeness is a very vague term, oftener used than understood, and often applied as a dress coat, to suit occasions, perhaps hide defects. Good manners instilled through good principles, as in the daily pleasant family scene above, form a solid groundwork for character, by means of happy associations; children thus taught, learn to apply the moral sense of their own accord, find it incorporated with all their ideas, ready on all occasions, and bestowing on ease and a charm, that mere external politeness seldom acquires!

loaded hands and aprons. Mr. Bordley liked to delay a little with his friends, over a well-cooled glass of Madeira, and a profusion of exquisite fruit. He liked also, at this moment, to give and receive the overflowings of the heart and fancy, in a frank and free interchange of good humor, or grave debate, or calm reflection, and he always found some who gladly remained with him. Mr. Bordley's manners were happily demonstrative and marked with peculiar candor; whether he indulged in playful sportiveness, philosophic inquiry, keen remark, or pious feeling, his actual meaning was ever in his words and his countenance, and those who conversed and listened, perceived with certainty that they had heard the truth and something worth remembering.

> "   * * * * * How could my tongue
> Take pleasure and be lavish in thy praise!
> How could I speak thy nobleness of nature!
> Thy open manly heart, thy courage, constancy,
> And inborn truth, unknowing to dissemble!"—ROWE.

The family at last dispersed to their several avocations, and Mr. Bordley to a cool seat and his book. There he remained abstracted from everything present, until summoned by the movements of others, to join in an evening walk with one, or an evening row on the water with another, or perhaps to take some others in the phaeton round his farm, to view his fields and improvements. On returning from these excursions, they found the tea-table prepared, sometimes, in extreme warm weather, placed on the "neat smooth shaven green," and abundantly supplied with every suitable luxury from "either India," and from a well stored dairy and larder; with every

variety and preparation of fruit, and with merriment warm
from the hearts of various ages! Sometimes, in the midst
of this gay clattering hilarity, the whole Lloyd family
would suddenly appear! The noise of their ten-oared barge
having been lost in that of tongues. Then was there an
accession of mirth and conviviality from those gay, good-
humored neighbors! Mrs. Lloyd (she was a Miss Tayloe,
of Virginia) never failing to supply her innocent jest and
drollery, and at parting, enjoining Mr. Bordley to return
to public life, and give them balls; that the farmer's life
had made him too serious, &c.

Such was the general mode of Mr. Bordley's summer
hours, an evening seldom passed without visits either given
or received; and the favoring moon was uniformly courted
for a lengthened enjoyment of converse after a sultry day.
If to the gorgeous, the ambitious, or the plodding inhabit-
ant of cities, such a life seems vacant, let him acknowledge
whether his own be happier!

> " How various his employments, whom the world
> Calls idle, and who justly in return
> Esteems that busy world an idler too!
> Friends, books, a garden, and perhaps his pen,
> Delightful industry enjoy'd at home,
> And nature in her cultivated trim,
> Dress'd to his taste, inviting him abroad—
> Can he want occupation who has these?
> Oh! friendly to the best pursuits of man,
> Friendly to thought, to virtue, and to peace,
> Domestic life in rural leisure pass'd."—COWPER.

Sunday was a "day of rest." It was marked by suitable
readings and reflection, and enlightening lessons to the
young. When the sky was clear and not too hot, and in-

dicated no near or distant gust, the carriage was ordered
across the river in a horse boat, and the family following
in a batteau, joined it and proceeded to the nearest church,
which was twelve miles distant. There, breathing forth
devout offerings of the heart in our beautiful liturgy, they
heard selections from the Book of books, and afterwards
listened to a wholesome plain discourse from their excellent
Parish Pastor, the Rev. Mr. John Gordon. This gentleman was a frequent guest amongst his parishioners, and
was often welcomed at Mr. Bordley's for days together,
particularly for part of the Christmas festival. His education, his office, and the guileless simplicity of his character, with his affectionate disposition, greatly won Mr. B.'s
regard—add to which, both liked an honest game of back-
gammon, and to converse with liberality and freedom on
general topics, and also, on that sacred theme which is to
"make men wise unto salvation."

Mr. Bordley's winter hours were marked by the same
views and pursuits as those of summer, allowing a larger
proportion of time to such as were sedentary. He was still
to be found giving his most earnest attention to whatever
lay within his sphere of duty. The weather must have
been inclement indeed, that could prevent his daily visit
to his farm; or his unvarying care for the welfare of his
people, in which latter branch of duty he was constantly
aided by his humane and judicious helpmate, ever ready
to adopt that good old-fashioned title, but never more so
than in promoting deeds of charity. Winter leisure allowed
him to gratify his taste for books of science and general
knowledge, while through the medium of newspapers,
magazines, and friendly correspondences, he kept up his

acquaintance with the state of the world, far and near, and his pen furnished him another intellectual variety. His pleasant turn for social amusement, willing to meet the advances of others, always found some of those lighter relaxations which the human mind requires, and in the good sense, sound principles, and uniformly cheerful temper of his wife, he possessed a companion who made the longest hours appear short. In winter he gave more attention to a subject mutually interesting to them both, viz., the education of their little daughter—to the age of thirteen she had no hired teacher,* and was fully prepared by her parents, to enter the highest class of the best Philadelphia school. Their parlor table was in winter to be seen covered with maps, slates, and divers volumes of instruction, and while the philosophic mind of the father endeavored to infuse into his pupils' memory some small portion of the abstruse sciences, history, geography, morality and religion principally devolved on the gentle and highly cultivated mind of the mother; but this subject opens a field of reflection too fertile for our limits!

And now approaches a period which led Mr. Bordley once more to an important remove and change of scene! From the time of his second marriage, he had occasionally passed several entire winters in Philadelphia, where their Union Street house was always ready for their reception. During these visits, he became attached to many of its inhabitants; delighted with its resources for knowledge; and reconciled, in some measure, to city habits—we cannot

---

* To this, one exception must be mentioned—she received private lessons in dancing, from the age of seven, whenever her parents visited the city. All the other usual accomplishments were not entered upon until her thirteenth year.

say more on this subject; for who, that has once fully enjoyed, with gratitude to the Great Parent of Nature, the
pure freedom and elegant case of the rural life, can ever
completely like the artificial restraints of a city?   Mr.
Bordley, however, was not a slave to mere habit; with his
enlightened mind, and fondness for intellectual improvements, he was sensible of the advantages that civilized life
obtains from these congregated masses of men; amongst
whom fair Science flourishes, and education fosters all that
is refined and most estimable in the human character—
and he now turned his thoughts towards a permanent remove to Philadelphia; partly to secure some of these advantages for his little daughter, partly to gratify her
mother's natural desire to be, in the decline of life, near
her son, and her early friends; and partly also, to remove
from within the precincts of slavery—a misfortune entailed
on his native State, which he never ceased to deplore!

On this subject Mr. Bordley had long and deeply pon-
dered; but, alas! it was a theme on which no reflection
could give relief; and the writer has often witnessed its
oppressive weight on his mind; not that he considered the
holding slaves as criminal, in those who were unhappily
born to the inheritence; but whether he gave the subject
a general and patriotic view, as repressing the energies of
the whole mass of people, and in time producing the moral
evils of false pride and listless retrograding indolence, or
whether he viewed its saddening difficulties, entailed by
our selfish predecessors in the government, for the purpose
of cultivating our noble lands, still, in every aspect, he
found it a national affliction, and turned from the revolt-
ing theme with a dismay proportioned to its invincibility.

His colored people were much attached to him; having always viewed him like a patriarchal father amongst them, they justly considered him their best friend. It was now, when preparing to leave them, that his difficulties arose. Owning them on all his Maryland farms, they were of course numerous; and to have liberated them all at once, would have been an injury to his compatriots; he could not take on his conscience the commotion and danger likely to ensue. He had only a choice of evils, and made the following arrangement.

He liberated a portion on each farm, by families, and as a reward for proven fidelity; others, favorite family domestics, he took to Pennsylvania, where they were bound for a term of years; others, on disposing of his lands to different purchasers, he sold to those purchasers for a term of years, after which they and their progeny were to be free; others he left with his sons, and his daughter Ross, from whom they were sure of receiving kind treatment.

After the death of his venerable sister, the last of his father's family, Mr. Bordley made preparations for his contemplated change of residence, and accomplished it in the autumn of 1791; resigning the beautiful Island estate, with its improvements and advantages, to his then bachelor son, Matthias.

Just before the journey, when his daughter, Mrs. Ross, was waiting to bid a last farewell to the family, from that scene of past happiness, a circumstance occurred, which we cannot avoid mentioning, though we can give no explanation of it; yet it is valuable as a proof of the confidence reposed in Mr. Bordley by General Washington.

12

At the time alluded to, an express brought a sealed packet from the President to Mr. Bordley; it contained some confidential communication that was never made known to the family; but it could not be forgotten, as it required Mr. B.'s absence from home, and delayed the approaching journey for some days.

At length, all obstacles removed, the last "good-by," the last shake of the hand, the "God bless you!" and the last "lingering look" given, they quitted this lovely spot, this happy home of the heart, and pursued "their silent way" towards Philadelphia. Various were the emotions and reflections of the party; and even Mrs. Bordley, who had the attractions of kindred and home to look forward to, yet fondly and gratefully owned that she experienced sorrow in quitting "the dear, the delightful Wye Island!"

And anon, all were snugly settled in Union Street; and the greetings of friends, the stir, the enterprise, and the spirited movements of a city, with the various consultations on various subjects, inquiries and arrangements with tutors, &c., &c., these things banished painful regrets, and soon completely and cheerfully engrossed the time and thoughts of the now re-established citizens.

Philadelphia was then, and for some years afterwards, the seat of the General Government; and may be said to have concentrated at that time more social attractions than have fallen to her lot, or to that of any of our cities, since the removal of Government to its own metropolis. Society there held its highest tone, and shone with all the most exalted excellencies and the most pleasing varieties of the human materials which formed it. It was then enriched by a large accession of well-educated strangers, driven by revolutionary terrors from the distinguished classes of every part of Europe; and by the learned, the honorable, the gay and the lovely, from all parts of our own dear country. The social principle was well understood; the domestic scene was enlivened and improved by the duty of hospitality to the "stranger," and the stranger in return, by grateful good-will and desire to please, converted that duty into a pleasure; whilst the simple but well-established forms of republican etiquette, appertaining to the order of all good government, taught men the mutual advantages to be derived from mutual respect.

During that period, Mr. Bordley's house became one of the favorite places of friendly resort to some amongst the excellent of all descriptions. Unostentatious good sense, and cheerfulness, and ease, rendered the dinners, suppers, balls, &c. at his house peculiarly attractive; besides which a constant evening circle was voluntarily assembled there— happy in the polished ease which they both found and reciprocated. There often met together foreign nobility and republican talents; the graces of the old world and simplicity of the new—with the learned and scientific of both—often a heterogeneous mixture! From the wily and elegant courtier, the ci-devant Bishop d'Autun, Tallyrand Perigord de Montmorenci, to the plain, rough, honest, and acute Secretary of State, Timothy Pickering; from the unpolished, timid, and retiring philosopher, Volney, to the polished, pleasant, persevering, and penetrating ambassador, Mr. Liston, (now Sir Robert,) &c.

Some time before settling in Philadelphia, Mr. Bordley was appointed by the President one of the Commissioners for receiving subscriptions to the Bank of the United States,* but his affairs in Maryland arbitrarily required his presence there at that time, and he could not consent to neglect them; and after meeting the other Commissioners once or twice, and giving some limited attention to the subject, he either silently declined acting further, or resigned his commission, it is not now recollected which. Had he been ambitiously disposed he probably would have acted otherwise; but, on removing to the seat of Government, he at once took occasion to let it be known that he was not desirous of office, and was allowed to cultivate the independent leisure he preferred; whilst at the same time his society was valued and his opinions respected by the "powers that be" of that day. The writer of this sketch greatly laments the loss of many interesting letters from some of the first men of the nation to Mr. Bordley, during various years, viz., from Washington, Jefferson, Hamilton, Wolcott, Cabot, &c. If these had been preserved, they might now throw some further light on the character we wish to depict. We have seen the letters referred to; but, alas! they are lost!

But we may trace Mr. Bordley's motive by his conduct: having long renounced politics, and shunned contention with men of the world, he now considered himself too far advanced in life to return to that forsaken career. He once remarked to an intimate friend, "they can be at no loss for younger men to fill their public offices—let me lay on the shelf." He never lost that love of independence which had influenced his whole life. We have some lines that he once gave the writer, not for the value of the

* His commission bears date "March 19, 1791."

poetry, but because "they are," he said, "as expressive of my own sentiments, as if I had written them." We cannot resist inserting them here:

> "While sordid souls are importuning Heav'n,
> To grant them riches ne'er to mortals giv'n;
> While some are anxious for their worldly fate,
> And wish to mount the lofty car of State;
> To Providence I'll offer one request—
> For void of this I never can be blest—
> Grant me, kind Heav'n! an independent mind,
> Above the vulgar meanness of mankind;
> No haughty Tyrants let me ever court,
> Nor for their favor with my honor sport:
> Let no mean action e'er my conduct stain,
> Altho' by it, I might a kingdom gain:
> I'd rather beg my bread from door to door,
> Than be a fawning sycophant to power—
> Oh! let me then reiterate my prayer,
> May mental independence be my share!"

We may, therefore, easily see why Mr. Bordley shunned party influence, and this not in political affairs only, but in all affairs whatever; he had no desire to become a leader, and was principled against implicit conformity to a party, for partial views.

But it did not accord with his character to be inactive, and he soon found that if pent up within the walls of a city, without a profession, he might sigh with Othello, "my occupation's gone!" He therefore turned again towards fields and meadows—his favorite themes, and purchased a fine farm in Chester County, about thirty miles from town, consisting of 360 acres of noble wood-crowned hills, and meadows well irrigated by clear trout streams. Here he thought to realize some improved agricultural views, with the aid of free white laborers, and within a few miles of

two thriving market towns; and he calculated on the
honest aims of a suitable superintendent, who engaged as
both tenant and director in his absence, this being intended
only for the amusement of six months of the year. This
farm he named *Como*, from a classical regard to the birth-
place of Pliny, one of his favorite ancients. After some
visits of preparation he took his family there in 1795, and
spent one pleasant summer, again under the shade of his
own woods; again enjoying the free delights of planting,
planning, devising, and directing, with animated hopes,
and an activity beyond his years.

But it was now the will of Providence to draw his career
towards its close. He perceived the approach of that painful disease which had terminated his father's life, and
gradually threatened his own. Traveling, therefore, became impossible, and he at once resigned in cheerful sub-
mission, yet not without a sigh, the pleasing projects he
had just entered on. Thenceforth he endeavored to restrain
the enthusiasm so prone to expatiate over the wide field
of nature in largely liberal schemes, and to content himself
with the winter comforts of the city, and be thankful that
he could yet remove to some rural retreat in its vicinity
for the summer months, where he might have his sufferings alleviated by the best medical aid, and his mind
amused by friendly society, and a varied supply of literature; now it was, particularly, that he was thankful for
the early habit of and fondness for reading, acquired in his
brother's office, as before alluded to: it was now become
invaluable.

And here it is impossible not to mention the satisfaction
which Mr. Bordley derived from the character and con-

duct of his step-son, John F. Mifflin, Esq. There was a solid and undeviating friendship between these two gentlemen, from the first of their acquaintance to the last. It was founded on mutual respect, and sustained by mutual good offices; the generous regard, in both sentiment and conduct of the step-father, was returned by the judicious and prompt professional aid of the step-son ; while each found in the other a companionable friend, in whose society they mutually gained pleasure and advantage; in whose honor and integrity they firmly and undoubtingly relied. Some traits of character strikingly similar, happily tended to confirm their reciprocal regard; these were the genuine spirit of independence; the search after enlightened truth, and firm adherence to sound principle; the open-hearted frankness of speech, guided by discretion; the love of general knowledge, and a cheerful, manly sprightliness, gilding the most lonely hours of domestic intimacy with a charm, derived from a conscious nobleness of motive, which time could not subdue; for time, in his development of character, riveted still closer the bonds of union between them, strengthening to the last Mr. Bordley's attachment to his younger friend, in whom he vested, before his decease, the entire management of his affairs, with unabated and well proved confidence; and who soothed his declining hours with the tender fidelity of a son.

It is a delightful encouragement to the human heart to reflect on such examples!

In the spring of 1800, his daughter, Mrs. Henrietta Maria Ross, removed to Chambersburg, in Pennsylvania, from whence she made her father frequent visits; always accompanied by some of her numerous and amiable children, who to the last contributed to soothe the declining years of their grandfather.

Mr. Bordley's winters were still passed as usual in alternating civilities with his friends and acquaintances, but these forming a large circle, his health obliged him gradually to withdraw from accepting invitations, though not from receiving company at home, and when collecting them around his festive board, his judicious assortment of characters thus met together; his cordial, frank hospitality, his unassuming, easy, good manners; making others happy and himself respected; still, and always secured the willing attendance of the guests selected. His evening circle of volunteers also became more certain, as he was always at home, and when his wife and daughter prepared the usual cups of tea or coffee for him, before entering on their evening engagements for balls, drawing-room, &c., they had the satisfaction of seeing an enlivening group around him, and that animated smile on his countenance, which gave them courage to leave him.

For the summers, Mr. B. secured a small retreat from city heats and fevers, on the west side of Schuylkill, a place then belonging to David Beveridge, opposite to Fairmount. This situation was not then so public as at present; it was in an agreeable neighborhood, amongst the pretty villas of Powelton, the Solitude, Eaglesfield, &c., and within a pleasant riding distance of the Woodlands, Belmont, Roxborough, &c., and so near the city, that those kindly interested in the several members of the family, made them frequent visits, without expecting any parade or display; it was in this modest little retreat that the friendly, kind-hearted Mrs. Liston declared "she found more snug rural comfort than anywhere else around."

There Mr. B. had his usual evening circle, his table covered with books and papers, &c.; and his mind, being too vigorous and active to be content with reading only, his pen here resumed its old habits, preparing, as subjects occurred, useful hints and suggestions " for others to improve upon." Such was his liberal view in giving to the world those little pieces on diversified subjects already mentioned, several of them the production of the leisure he now found. Having learned, with great satisfaction, that the essays on farming, published at different times, had been productive of good effects, he now formed the idea of collecting them in one volume, and improved by subsequent experience and additional observations. This collection was published by Thomas Dobson, in 1799. It has gone through three large editions, and we are told that another is now wanted. It has received very respectable commendation from the critics and from the scientific of the old world,* and, what is still better, it has been of service to the new world—that portion which we are so happy as to call our own country. Could he have foreseen that his country would one day acknowledge itself benefited by his exertions in what he considered her best interests, how his benevolent heart would have thrilled! Yes! he would have said, " I am rewarded." The hope of aiding some few of her nobly independent sons of the soil, was his only aim in publishing that work. It was undertaken at a period when his disease was far advanced upon him; but that hope supported him in perseverance, under the most excruciating pains, ofttimes so torturing that his family would entreat him to desist and take rest,

---

* Dr. Willich—which see.

but he would resume his pen again and again, with this
and similar expressions: "No! I cannot stop; Americans
must learn to know the value of agriculture, and if I can
expedite or smooth the way to them, I must do it!"

May Americans indeed learn to appreciate that noble
science, and to connect with it every manly, moral and
immortalizing excellence!

John Beale Bordley desired this for them, with the first
and the last wishes of his heart; and it was not alone for
the profit they might derive from it; it was closely connected, in his mind, with their virtue, happiness, and
independence.

They possess the field for cultivating these. May they
cherish and preserve them forever!

Five summers were passed as above described, at Beveridge's place on the Schuylkill. In 1801 he was too ill to
leave town; in 1802 he again sighed for the reviving air
of the country, and took a place in the same neighborhood,
a mile higher up the river, to which he again returned in
the summer of 1803—the last time he beheld the cheering
face of Nature!

In the following winter, the disease became more powerful; the poor frame yielded; on January 26th, 1804, the
spirit sought its rest in "the bosom of its Father and its
God!"

Having now closed the outline of events in Mr. Bordley's
life, there seems still something wanting. Perhaps it is
natural to desire a more intimate view of the manners and
peculiarities of one with whom we have been so long
abiding; and as this little sketch is designed for some who

have never seen this, their respected ancestor, let us try to place him before them!

In stature Mr. Bordley was five feet ten inches; his limbs stout and well set, indicative of strength, and well proportioned; his carriage was, until bent with age and pain, remarkably erect, but not stiff; his deportment at once pleasing and commanding; his hair dark, but not black; his complexion a clear and ruddy brown; his forehead high, full and fair; his eyes dark gray; his eyebrows thick and arched. His countenance was the honest index of his feelings, and like them, controlled by good sense, but not by artifice. As he was prone to be pleased with others and interested in all around him, so a certain lighted-up smile of good humor rewarded those who were the occasion of it; its usual expression, as his usual state of mind was placid and benevolent: but those same features could be roused with just resentment to a look that few would desire to be the cause of repeating. Perhaps it was, in part, this weapon provided by nature, which, judiciously employed, kept him in harmony with all his acquaintances; for it was remarkable that he had no quarrels. His well-known benevolence and kindness of heart opened the door to reciprocal feelings, whilst his equally well-known aversion to error stood like a sentinel to guard against improper intrusion, or that "too great familiarity" which, the proverb justly remarks, "breeds contempt."

Mr. Bordley, through life, was remarked for the good manners and ease of a well-bred man. This, in him, was the "second nature" produced by early good "habit;" no one could more loathe every species and degree of affectation. Yet it was a habit which, in him, grew out of more than the consequences of associating with good company. It is true that Annapolis, where the first half of his life was passed, possessed, in the circle he frequented, a refined and elegant society; but there was also a charm in his manners, which arose in the heart, varying naturally with circumstances; it was fostered and guided by native good sense, constant observation, and a sincere veneration for the principles of Christianity as a rule of life. His look and air seemed to acknowledge "kindred" with every human being. He gave a cordial and heartfelt respect to every species of merit, no matter where found. He never lost an opportunity of endeavoring to do it justice, either in words or actions, and this not for parade or any sinister motive, because it sometimes happened that his tribute or justice to one was not pleasing to others, or might be mis-construed by them; but he seemed to make every one's case his own, and willing to take it for granted that others were as glad to be just as he himself was. In his domestic circle, nothing more disturbed him than those thoughtless denunciations so apt to arise amongst the chatterers of the world, without investigation, and founded lightly on the first vague report of idlers! This was so well under-stood that, in his presence, anything appertaining to petty scandal was sure to be whispered, often drawing from him, with an arch smile, the remark, "Aye? are you certain that's right? Come, let me hear it!" No one better relished a jest, or lively play of fancy, than he did; he would also tolerate a little ridicule, but his aversion to error was on principle, and therefore relented and mingled with com-passion when directed against "frail fellow-mortals"—(his own expression.) He was not, however, one particle the less aware of the existence of evil in the world. His candor in cheerfully acknowledging himself wrong, and his alike open frankness in detecting the faults or foibles of even his best friends, were evidences of his penetration and discrimination well known to all his intimates, few of whom, very few, ever shrunk from his sportive raillery, however tender the spot it touched. They knew too well the guileless and affectionate nature of the "inward man," and knew that it rested with themselves to make his sense of truth and justice a benefit to themselves, or otherwise.

In recollecting this trait of character in Mr. Bordley, we cannot avoid being struck by a similar one in his father, as drawn by the preacher to whom we before referred, who says of Thomas Bordley, Esq., in 1726: "He was a very rigid lover of justice, insomuch that he would not spare his best friends, when they committed any transgression within his cognizance."

Perhaps it may be asked whether Mr. Bordley was equally willing to be subjected to the test of other persons' judgments and opinions? We answer, Yes! But they must abide by their own motive. If malevolence, envy, low pride, vanity, or impertinence, were at the bottom of their suggestions, no one could more clearly detect the false ground, or better defend himself, not always by retort, but by that species of self-guardianship which belongs to behavior and conduct. If, on the contrary, the detection of his errors or mistakes arose from pure motives, such as might playfully face the light, or came clothed with the "modesty of fearful duty," or the warmth of proven friend-

13

ship, or with the honest indignation of one who considered himself injured, and sought explanation, in all such cases he considered himself a gainer, inasmuch as he had obtained a glimpse of that truth of things, which, appear wherever and however it might, he estimated as a portion of the "pearl above all price;" and he felt at once thankful to the being who had contributed to enlighten him, whether it were a little child, or even a poor slave.* Numerous are the instances in which he thankfully permitted the intimacy of friendship to put him in the right; and none need fear doing so but those whose own mistaken views made them cowards. In fact, his love of virtue was superior to his love of self; and he truly and fervently wished others to be all that he wished to be himself, and that in this way friendship might be mutual and yet independent. Those who had not strength of character enough to think or to be anything of themselves; whose trembling pride was ever on the alarm, and who feared doing justice by others, lest it should depreciate from or entangle themselves; with such he could have nothing in common, either in heart or mind, excepting the mere wants of poor humanity; and though they might and did receive his sympathy for such wants, yet could he give them no mu-

---

* This is not hypothesis—the writer remembers many, very many instances of this trait of character. One or two may suffice. He was in the habit of conversing freely, at times, with his most intelligent blacks, and has often acknowledged himself instructed by some of their remarks, and their untaught, native powers of reasoning. We have heard them say to him, to rouse his attention, "Ah! now massa wrong—massa say he love right way—ma' he no listen to 'um now!"—and he would become all patience in listening! He would often yield to the sarcasms of his sensible Scotch neighbor, Mr. Adam Gray, and laughingly exclaim, "Ah, hah! Mr. Adam! there you got the better of me!" &c., &c.

tual accordance, save pity and civility. Amongst such as
these might be found some, doubtless, who would endeavor
to stigmatize him as a proud man !

It is hard for the majority of mankind to understand
their brethren, or themselves, from the conceited Pharisee
who "thanked God he was not like other men," down to
the humble "sinner" who felt most for his own infirmities.
Yet it is the sacred duty of all to endeavor to be just.
There is but one rule of right ; but numerous and innu-
merable ways lie open to each individual for applying that
rule to circumstances and characters. Thank Heaven!
there have been, and still are some few, a noble few, who
can put a generous construction on these matters, and who
go by the "spirit"—that blessed spirit ! and not by the
mere "letter" of the law.

It is difficult to describe such a character as Mr. Bordley's with accuracy and force, yet without in some way
"o'erstepping the modesty of nature."

To say that it was benevolent, vigorous, and original,
are just divisions of its leading features ; yet in each of
these were delicate shades, rendered interesting by characteristic peculiarities, not so easily described.

Thus, in his benevolence, there was the union and accord
of native, constitutional kind feeling, with a high acquired
sense of the beauty of order, and duties of a rational
being.

In his vigor, there was nothing of the proud spirit of
dominion, nor of overbearingness.

In his originality, there was neither whimsy nor self-
conceit. He chose to pursue the dictates of his own mind;

but he equally chose to keep that mind enlightened and
subdued by the immutable principles of truth, as he found
them revealed to us by divine authority. In this, we
conceive, consisted his strongest point of character—that
while endeavoring to purify and exalt the living principle
within his bosom, by considerations on the true dignity of
man, he yet felt and acknowledged himself far from the
goal, and roused himself to perpetual efforts towards it.

He was favored by nature with a strong mind, and very
early showed a reflecting habit and a self-possession uncommon for his years; and apparently the native growth
of his mind; for he was left much to himself, and free
from any control, excepting that of custom and his own
good sense. As he advanced in life, this happy disposition
to follow what was right in the sight of God and of his
own conscience, mellowed his passions, naturally warm, to
a noble moderation, and a beautiful consistency of moral
conduct, and led him also to prefer happiness to splendor, and
the consciousness of rectitude to the world's applause.

The prevailing turn of his mind may be termed philosophical; but he made no pretensions to a character, and
neither acted " to be praised of men" while living, nor yet
to furnish his biographer with a brilliant display of qualities and honors. Indeed, it may be seen that he ran
counter to this common course, and avoided many of those
gifts of fortune which others seek.*   Had he been ambitious
of worldly honors, he was already high on the ladder of
public distinction, and might have attained the highest
rewards from popularity; but he voluntarily resigned

---

* This was so well known and understood in his family and amongst his
friends, as to be a standing joke with them against him; but his philosophy
contented itself with smiling in turn at them!

them. Had he desired riches, fortune there also was kind, and he might have accumulated great wealth, had accumulation been his aim. Had he wished to be esteemed a learned man, he had only to indulge and fix a natural propensity, and the object was soon his own—his native powers would have held him out in anything he chose to aim at; but he desired no distinction beyond the respect he actually received, and this he hoped still to derive from the steady and conscientious discharge of those duties which his high calling as a sentient and reasonable being, and still more as a Christian, demanded from him. These he conceived he could better discharge in a private than in a public career; and who shall doubt the wisdom of his choice, seeing, as he saw, the dangers to which the love of popularity leads, the evil passions it kindles even in the best dispositions, and the disappointment which in some shape or other generally attends it :

> "O you! whom vanity's light bark conveys
> On Fame's mad voyage by the wind of praise:
> With what a shifting gale your course you ply,
> Forever sunk too low, or borne too high!
> Who pants for glory, finds but short repose—
> A breath revives him, or a breath o'erthrows."
> —Pope's Horace.

Although desiring no individual honors or distinctions from the world, few men could be more conscious of the true dignity to which human nature is called, or of the high aims and noble privileges of the human soul—that glorious principle which can sustain man under all the privations incident to his frail existence here—can give him equal triumph whether on a throne or in a dungeon—

13*

and direct its aspirations above the callous cruelties of evil spirits in disguise, to that blessed "haven of rest" where joy reigns forever.

As in Mr. Bordley's love of knowledge there was no ostentation, so was there nothing selfish or exclusive in it. No vain overestimate of his own acquisitions made him needlessly communicative, or solemnly dogmatical; no false delicacy or fear of misconstruction wrapped him in silent reserve; and no puerile ambition, or pitiful endeavor to supplant others, induced him to take the lead in conversation. Believing all useful information, of whatever kind, a common stock, and every just sentiment and opinion as seed sown, like the "mustard seed," for reclaiming the world from error, and an advance, however small, towards the kingdom of truth and happiness, his honest desire was that knowledge might be rendered diffusive, and that he, as an humble agent, might both give and receive towards its universal promulgation. He was remarkable, in all his transactions, for the pleasure he took in enlightening the ignorant. Not an artisan of any description, not a poor beggar, nor a little child ever came into communication with him without receiving some remarks, in the form of pleasant hints, which they might remember to their own advantage. This same principle was the basis of his small early pieces on public sentiment, agriculture, &c., and of his well-known easy habit of cheerfully communicating his ideas, so as to please all, great or small, polished or unpolished, young or old, whom he found capable of receiving them.

We recollect many instances of his manly composure and friendly firmness in strengthening those whose situations claimed his sympathy. Some of his own words are before us, as in a letter to a young friend who had lost his father, he says :

" * * * * We ought to be surprised at nothing, much less ought we to be astonished at common events. That which we all look for, may be met with composure and a philosophic firmness. A sedate and religious mind will, on every stroke of affliction, naturally resort to that Being who alone affords solid comfort. With pleasure I reflect I have often experienced it ! I offer you my services—the affectionate regard I had for your father commands them," &c.

To a sensible friend, in reduced circumstances, who was industriously endeavoring to repair them by establishing an exchange coffee-house in Baltimore, he addresses, in one of his letters, the following encouraging language :

" * * * * Still more animating, however, was the inclosure of the two letters, which convey approbation, in men of character, of your noble endeavors to confirm your independence. And this same L——n is still the same L——n, approved by his friends, and men of character! It is the sentiments and manners that declare the gentleman ; in a free country, where there is not the idle pride of a Spaniard—be his employment what it may—for it cannot be immoral—he is still himself," &c.

Not long after removing to the Eastern Shore, Mr. Bordley had the happiness to restore peace and harmony between two estimable families, where he was equally intimate. It was in 1774. Two gentlemen residing not far from Easton, who had married sisters, on some occasion,

now unknown, came to a "deadly breach" which long kept
them at variance. Mr. Bordley, feeling their entire confidence in him, wrote to each of them in a strain of mingled
scolding, raillery, and a humor peculiar to himself. The
letters are now before us, but do not admit of quotation,
and are too long to insert entire. The gentlemen knew
his impartiality, his sound judgment, and the excellence of
his heart; such a representation, therefore, coming from
him, was irresistible, and the wound was healed. "Blessed,"
indeed, are such privileges!

Mr. Bordley had native talents for the fine arts, but his
graver duties did not permit him to cultivate them. Thus,
with a strong and decided taste for painting, he never
took instruction, even in drawing. We have, however, a
landscape painted by him in oil colors, the view from his
house at Wye, that proves our assertion of native talent;
it was his first and only experiment with the brush, and it
may be said to at least equal some of the first attempts of
those who were, afterwards, great painters. His fondness
for this charming art was shown by the fostering attention
he gave it in others. A young artist was sure of his sympathy and patronage.

His feeling and enjoyment of music was also marked,
and, indeed, exquisite. A touching melody, or well executed melodious harmony, would draw tears of pleasure to
his eyes.

We would not be understood to say that his taste
included all the beaux arts equally. We are not aware
that it extended to poetry, although he was acquainted
with all the best poets in our language; but he had no
strong natural bias towards it. His mind, as we have

before said, was of a mathematical and philosophical cast. It was formed by its Almighty Author with a great proportion of natural good feeling, capable of being wrought up into many excellencies; but it was not the fashion of the world in those days to diversify and enfeeble the powers of the mind by superficial embellishments and enervating refinements. Men aimed at being substantial, stout and steady, and Mr. Bordley's conduct, in all respects, proved that he disdained to hold forced pretensions, and claimed no rights beyond the plain truth of things.

Mr. Bordley had a truly pious mind; he cherished a deep-seated sentiment of devotion, commingling with and directing all his other principles. He revered the blessed revelation of God's will, and adored His mercy in giving light and hope to the world in His Son Jesus Christ. He delighted in the beautiful ethics of Christianity, and made them his rule of life. He was well acquainted with the Scriptures, from his youth up. Amongst other proofs of this, is a familiar letter to one of his brothers, in which he says:

1756. "* * * * I am extremely fond of the Universal History, but I cannot yet read it with study. It however gives me very great satisfaction, and has a strong influence on my religious affections. I observe especially it is much in favor of the Scriptures, and makes the dry narrative of the Old Testament very agreeable and intelligible. I shall finish it at Harvest, where I shall take it under a shady mulberrie."*

He often in later life was fond of indulging in a quiet conversation or a friendly letter, where his heart could

---

* On his farm near Joppa.

freely unbend without incurring the charge of either ostentation or presumption, in unfolding his views of this solemn subject. He claimed the right in this, as in other objects of inquiry, of forming his own opinions, coming to the investigation with an humble mind, conscientiously seeking the truth. One of those leading principles which gave his mind some of its tone and power, was his aversion to prejudice. He scrupulously endeavored to keep it free from this debasing influence; for he considered it a bar to all improvement, and an enemy to that beautiful system of amelioration which our Saviour left to the world. On this subject he used to say: "To see things as they are, and to bring things to what they ought to be, must be the desire of every true Christian."

> "Those who have eyes to see, let them see:
> Those who have ears to hear, let them hear."

But while he thus endeavored to regulate himself and the young minds subject to his control, he was equally scrupulous in not wounding the feelings or opposing the opinions of others.

His satisfaction in perusing the Bible, and particularly the New Testament, increased in his later years, and then, when pain and disease were undermining his poor frame, were to be seen the soothing and blessed effects of an according and faithful spirit, preparing to receive better things than "eye hath yet seen, or ear heard."

Mr. Bordley's family, as has been seen, were all, for many generations, of the Protestant Episcopal Church. To this church he always belonged, and was fond of attending its public worship, always holding a pew in that

nearest to his residence, and supporting by his countenance
and example that happy bond of order and good fellowship
which he considered essential to all the blessings of civilization. With his excellent pastor on the Eastern Shore,
Mr. John Gordon, he often corresponded.* He was fond
of writing occasionally on the leading principles of religion; and although in some points differing from others,
he made it an affair of conscience not to intrude his peculiar views on those differing from him. His mind was too
liberal, and too truly humble, (in a Christian sense,) to
suppose he had either the right or the power to "judge"
others, or to judge for others, and he allowed the same
freedom of opinion which he claimed. He endeavored to
promote the one great leading principle, the pious spirit,
wherever his duty on the subject was evident, beginning
in his own family, as, for instance, in the instructions he
early gave to his little daughter, when she accompanied
him in his visits to the farm. He then, as at other times,
availed himself of opportunities, as they arose, to awaken
her young mind to a sense of the power, wisdom, and
goodness of Providence, sometimes remarking how the
tender grain put forth its leaves and was protected,
&c., thence leading her to reflect on who gave the
seed power to grow, and how the same Being thus supplies
us with the "daily bread" we ask for, but which is not to
be obtained without effort and exertion on our part, as
evinced by the necessity of cultivating the ground;
thence describing the like necessity for enriching and preparing our minds, which are to produce a nobler kind of

* He once wrote a sermon, and sent it to that clergyman, who expressed
great approbation of it.

bread, and must be carefully cleared from the evil weeds
so prone to spring up everywhere and "choke the good
seed." Thus training her to a habit of reflection on her
duties, as our Saviour himself did, by remarks drawn from
the simple and beautiful phenomena of nature; referring
her to his divine precepts and authority, thus instructing
her in a twofold sense, and winning a delighted ear to
engraft those perfect precepts indelibly, by grateful love
and strong association on her mind, and thus uniting her
admiration of nature indissolubly with the love and adora-
tion of nature's Great Creator.

These conversations, warm from the heart of a parent,
became more and more instructive and delightful to the
young pupil as they enlarged to suit her expanding capacity, blending the father's practical and philosophical illus-
trations with the serious reading, self-examination and
prayer, held in the retirement of the mother's chamber.
Happy the child so taught! Blessed the parents so
teaching!

In a character such as Mr. Bordley's, where piety
formed the heart of the system, and generosity a strong
feature, charity is so naturally a concomitant that it seems
almost needless to name it, yet we will mention one of the
judicious modes of exercising it which he practiced throughout life. This was by giving encouraging attentions, and
small timely aids in the way of loans, to such as needed,
especially to young artists and mechanics. "This," he
used to remark, "was calculated to keep up their spirit,
and a decent pride, with the love of order; and that more
was to be done for them by teaching them to help themselves, than would be by large free donations." He con-

trived generally to hear of or find out such opportunities ; and many were the instances, wherever he resided, of his having promoted those in their humblest beginnings, who afterwards rose to eminence in their vocation. And let it here be mentioned, to the credit of poor human nature, that he generally (alas! there must be always exceptions) perceived some gratitude in return. It has often happened, within the writer's knowledge, that these acts of kindness have been only brought to light by the objects of them coming, after a while, to express their thanks, or sending some little present to the same effect.

Mr. Bordley was probably brought to this plan by early observations on life, for he was early observant to good purpose. Amongst what he called his " scribblings," we have lately met with one on the back of an old account-book, which contains the following sensible thoughts, set down for his private satisfaction. They were written about 1765, and below them is a note of a later period, stating that "The above reflections were occasioned by the ingratitude of a relation, on whom I had bestowed a considerable value." They may be considered as a specimen of his mode of reasoning on conduct :

" When you intend a generous or charitable act, make not the least promise. If by accident you cannot perform it, you will never be forgiven. If you do perform it fully to your own intention and promise, it is odds but the person benefited had figured to himself much greater advantages to accrue to him under that promise, than you ever expressed or intended. Or if he does not, the wonder will be great if some of his friends (as they would call themselves) do not find great fault.

14

"Give without promise; give simply and purely, with a firm spirit and on good reflection, and only to those few who are actually and most certainly in distress; and let them know they are not obliged to you. If there is any kind of obligation attending it, is it not more a loan than a gift? Give only when it is necessary, and you do but your duty to a fellow-traveler. A sense of having done your duty carries with it its own reward; and I know of no sensation so agreeable as what arises from such a reflection, that you should be permitted, by the opportunity thrown in your way, of doing so good an act as the relief of a fellow-creature, and perhaps many depending on him."

We have been restrained, throughout this imperfect sketch, from saying as much as we know we might, and as we wished, by our long-established respect for the love of simplicity in the character before us. We have all along felt as though his sainted spirit was hovering over our pen, endeavoring to check its ardent flow; to repress, as was his parental practice when in this life, each extravagance of thought, or exuberance of expression.

Would that some more privileged and enlightened mind could do his memory justice!

Our feeble effort is now done; and we think we cannot better conclude than by copying the inscription from his tomb, in St. Peter's Church-yard, Philadelphia. It was composed by his valued friend, John F. Mifflin, Esq., whose character for independence and truth gives it additional value.

" THIS MONUMENT IS ERECTED

TO THE MEMORY OF

JOHN BEALE BORDLEY, ESQUIRE.

WHO DIED JAN. 26. 1804.

AGED 76 YEARS 11 MONTHS.

OF PROBITY AND INTEGRITY UNBLEMISHED—

AS A PHILANTHROPIST, PATRIOT, AND MAN.

EQUALED BY FEW,

EXCELLED BY NONE."

www.ingramcontent.com/pod-product-compliance
Lightning Source LLC
Chambersburg PA
CBHW021114020726

47500CB00003B/759